THE EMERALD RING

DARA GIRARD

ISBN: 978-1949764222

THE EMERALD RING

ILORI PRESS BOOKS, LLC

P.O. Box 10332

Silver Spring, MD 20914

www.iloripressbooks.com

Gaining Interest

Careless Rapture

Dangerous Curves

Familiar Stranger

It Happened One Wedding

Unexpected Pleasure

Midnight Promise

Sweet Temptation

Always and Forever

Truly Yours

Clifton Sisters

The Sapphire Pendant

The Amber Stone

The Emerald Ring

Fortune Brothers

A Tempting Proposal

A Seductive Arrangement

Novels

Honest Betrayal

The Daughters of Winston Barnett

Remember My Name

Illusive Flame

Winterwood Lane

PROLOGUE

DELAWARE EARLY 1900S

The pain came as a surprise, but it wasn't unwelcome. Wynette Clarise Martin winced and shifted her position on the hard wooden chair knowing she'd find no comfort no matter what position she eventually found. She hadn't known she was pregnant when she left her husband seven months ago for an amazing deal her uncle (she was never sure that there was any real blood relations between her mother and this man, but called him Uncle just the same) had told her about. Her husband had been wary, but Wynette had seen no other way they could make it to America. She dreamed of finding a place for them and starting a new life. Although she had attended school, she did not finish and dropped out at fifteen. She began working full-time with her mother who made her living as a seamstress. Her uncle told her that with her sewing skills, (she had acquired her mother's exceptional skill at being able to sew anything she saw perfectly) she could make a good living in America and that he had a contact. Wynette agreed to going to America and her uncle made all the travel arrangements.

She'd arrived in Miami, Florida in the spring, and was met by a woman, whose name was given to her by her uncle. The woman took her to a small hotel, and told her that her employer would be coming for her in a couple of days. She had no way to send news to her husband. Over the next several weeks, Wynette found herself working in dingy basements, backrooms, and other hovels, all the while having to work on various garments given to her. She spent most of her time sewing different items, from dresses to shirts to trousers, and getting paid 'piece meal' wages per item. She kept the money hidden by sewing them into her personal undergarments, which she wore at all times. They offered to keep her wages for her, but she didn't trust them.

Then one morning, without any warning, she was awaken early, before light, and bundled up into a van along with several other women. She was driven several miles, the journey taking more than a day, and ended up being left with a family and told that they were now her new employers. A finely dressed couple, Mr. and Mrs. Emery who had smiling faces, skin the color of chocolate milk and cold eyes.

Mr. Emery showed her a piece of paper, while his hand tried to wander where it shouldn't, and said that she owed them for her transportation and room and board, and would have to work for them for at least ten years. Although Wynette could read, she did not understand all that was written on the paper, and when she asked for a copy, Mr. Emery said she would get it when her contract was up. It was soon after that Wynette found out she was pregnant. Delighted by the news she eagerly told her new employers, hoping it would soften their hearts or at least give her a reprieve to return home, even briefly, but she'd been wrong. Instead Mrs. Emery's eyes turned even colder and Wynette's work load increased.

With the precious spare moments she could find, hidden away in the basement of the Emery's house, Wynette wrote many letters. First to her uncle (hoping he could help her) and then to her husband (desperate to share the news of their baby), but as the months passed with no reply from either of them, Wynette knew the letters had never been sent or had been intercepted. And she feared she'd never see the sweet face of her husband ever again. He'd been right to be wary and she wished she'd listened to him. But, as if he'd known they'd be parted, he'd left her with a piece of himself and it helped her to endure. In the day she thought of him and at night she imagined his hands touching her arms, touching her belly with a smile dancing on his lips; she imagined his arms wrapped around her, keeping her safe in the shelter of his embrace as they lay together in bed. At times it felt as if he were there as if she could hear his voice. For the past several months the days had been filled with waiting. Waiting to see him again, waiting for the baby to come.

Now the waiting was over, the arrival was imminent. Wynette glanced at the stack of dresses then looked at her watch. She was ahead of schedule but that didn't mean she could be slack. She took a deep breath as another tinge of discomfort struck her, but she dealt with it as stoically as she'd dealt with everything in her nineteen years. Like leaving school to help her mother full-time with her many orders since her mother's work kept them clothed and fed or handling her mother's unexpected passing.

At first she'd married her husband so she wouldn't be alone. He'd seemed to appear just when she needed him with no one else from her parish knowing much about him or his people, but to her surprise she'd quickly grown to love him. But love was not enough to live on and life was hard and making a living wage a struggle, so she'd written to her uncle. She'd never dreamed that although she loved to sew she would be doing it for ten hours a day, six days a week, alone in a room with one window too high up to look through.

Be calm. I am with you.

Wynette ran the material through the sewing machine with a slight smile, feeling the comfort of her lover's presence. She knew the sound of the machine would be what her baby knew. Its rhythmic motion like a lullaby.

She quickly, but efficiently, finished her last task, beads of sweat pooling on her forehead from the present physical labor and the anticipation of the one to come.

She lifted herself from the chair and walked over to the door, rubbing her back hoping to ease the tension, then knocked on the locked door, signaling that she was done.

It wasn't opened immediately as usual. Usually, Mr. or Mrs. Emery waited by the door at a certain hour ready to take the finished garments and leave. She feared that perhaps this time no one was there. She cast an eye on the old twin bed in the corner. She didn't want to have her baby there. She knocked again.

The door swung open. Mrs. Emery pursed her lips and said, "You're finished already?"

Wynette nodded and wiped the sweat from her forehead. "Yes, and my time has come."

Mrs. Emery glanced down at Wynette's swollen belly in disgust. Her disgust had been growing more evident each day, each month as the baby took hold of Wynette's petite form and molded it into something new.

"Are you sure?"

She nodded again. "Quite sure."

"Take a seat." Mrs. Emery motioned to the only chair in the room, the one behind the sewing machine. "I'll get you some water."

The last thing Wynette wanted was to be behind that

wretched machine again. She took a deep breath, determined to keep her tone low and respectful. "Thank you, but I don't need water right now. I need—"

The door closed in her face. She heard the lock engage. Wynette rested a hand against the wall and lowered her head. She would not panic. She had time.

But the glass of water did not come. And the pain increased. She banged on the door again.

The door opened.

Wynette took a deep breath, gasped between contractions and said, "Please, I need to go to the hospital."

"The doctor is on his way. You shouldn't be standing up in your condition anyway. " Mrs. Emery motioned to the bed. "You can rest there." She walked past her and set the glass on the ground.

Wynette didn't argue, carefully lowering herself on the edge of the bed. "But—"

"Has your water broken yet?"

"I'm sorry?"

"Have you wet yourself?"

"No."

"Good." She folded her arms. "Don't look at me that way. You're lucky I'm being as considerate as possible." She narrowed her eyes. "I know what you are. I know what you did."

The woman was mad, paranoid. Wynette had suspected as much the first time she'd seen her but she knew it even more now. No matter how many times she'd repeated it over the past several months Mrs. Emery refused to believe her, but she would say it again until she did. "I was never with your husband."

"We will soon see the proof."

Don't argue. Her husband's voice said to her. *I am with you. Focus on being a mother to our child now.*

A renewed strength filled her and almost without knowing what she was doing, as if she was being led, she moved to the side of the bed and got down on her knees.

Good, breathe with each movement. Your body knows the rest.

"What are you doing?" Mrs. Emery said.

Wynette didn't reply, she closed her eyes and centered herself, letting her body move with the waves of pain, letting it do its natural dance of bringing forth life.

"At least get up in the bed, don't just squat there."

Breathe, breathe, breathe.

Wynette breathed and moaned; she breathed and groaned. She thought she screamed but she wasn't sure, she focused on her husband—calling her, calming her, soothing her, loving her. She wasn't alone. Waves and waves of pain—biting, agonizing, terrifying then....then relief.

My brave darling.

The baby was out. Alive and well. She wrapped him up, but before she could hold him close Mr. Emery arrived with another man behind him. She could tell by their expressions what they had in mind.

"No!"

He snatched the baby from her arms while the other man placed something over her mouth.

And once more she heard her love's voice. *Be strong my love. I will avenge you.*

THE PRESENT

CHAPTER 1

MID 2000S

She wouldn't tell anyone.

Michelle Clifton stared at the notice in her left hand while drumming the fingers on her right against the impressive oak desk in her downtown office, searching her mind for the right response. She wanted to rip the certified letter into shreds. Crumple it into a ball, soak it with gasoline and torch it.

But somehow that still didn't feel good enough. Nothing seemed right to douse the rage she felt crawling over her skin, burning her heart. They were trying to ruin her.

Michelle set the letter down on the desk and took a deep breath. No, a hot, reckless temper was her youngest sister Jessie's territory. She was the cool one. The one who used her head, who'd learned the heart could be one's greatest betrayer. No, she wouldn't get angry and she wouldn't tell anyone that she wasn't getting her office lease renewed. No one needed to know that she may have to move her business elsewhere. No, no one needed to know because she wasn't moving anywhere. They wouldn't force her out.

As the owner of the Clifton Center for Business and Enterprise—CCBE for short—the location in the exclusive Winfield Building and its fabulous view of the downtown area and Catlon Bay in Randall County, Maryland had been ideal not just for her image—it screamed wealth and success and had clients and customers flocking to her—but for the people she sought to help. Getting to the prime location by either car or public transport was a breeze. Finding another location with the same advantages wouldn't be easy or as financially possible, but of course the Winfields knew that and didn't care.

No, she wouldn't tell anyone that her in-laws were trying to force her out. The powerful Winfields were a worthy adversary. She felt almost flattered that they somehow still saw her as a threat. There was no other reason they wanted to get rid of her. They owned numerous real estate properties, a lucrative construction business both in the US and abroad, a distribution center, a fashion line and several warehouses. In comparison, she was as threatening as a mosquito on the ass of an elephant. But for some reason they didn't think so.

Michelle touched the corner of the letter and slowly spun the paper around, listening to the soft whisper of sound as it shifted on the desk. There was a hidden motive here. They had left her alone for years after James had left. *What did they truly want?* She stopped spinning the letter, folded it up and placed it back in its envelope. She would have to find out before another notice came. No one in her company needed to know about her in-law's involvement, it would only cause them to worry. She was a single woman but all of her employees and contractors had families who depended on her. Depended on her to keep CCBE operating and profitable.

She would handle this situation on her own just as she had everything else she'd faced in life. It was better that way. Less messy and emotional. It kept her in control and over the past several years she'd learned that control was everything. She would always control the story she told and if she couldn't...she would leave blank spaces for speculation and never fill in the details. That had its power. Mystery was an excellent weapon.

And she knew there was plenty of mystery that surrounded her. Nobody knew why her marriage had broken up or where her estranged husband, James, was. Nobody knew why she'd remained in the office complex on the eighth floor that he'd given her only a year after they'd married. "It's yours," she remembered him saying when he'd removed his hands from her eyes and shown her the sprawling office layout. Even when he'd left he'd promised that the space would always be hers.

Clearly he'd lied.

Michelle leaned back in her seat, briefly glancing out at a boat bobbing along the calm waters of the bay on that cool summer day. She wouldn't go down without a fight. She'd spent too much of her life building up her business and making it a success. The Winfields had not wanted her as an in-law and she'd dealt with their subtle insults both before and after her marriage, but she'd grown stronger since then.

She'd lost her parents, her sisters had moved out and married, her husband had left her and all she had was her business. A cold smile filled with determination touched her lips. She'd hang on with bloody knuckles if need be. It was the principle of it. They didn't need the space.

They owed her. *He* owed her. She wouldn't try to find him. She didn't care where he was. She didn't need him. She didn't need anyone. Besides, she wouldn't stoop so low as to beg him to talk to his family to reverse this decision. She would face Martha Winfield herself. The woman who had once believed that Michelle was good enough for her grandson and now had changed her mind. Martha had been one of the few who'd been her champion, this notice felt like a betrayal. Now the Winfields could gloat that they'd been right all along. She wasn't one of them. 'Not quite their sort'.

Michelle frowned. Having to face that truth would be hard to swallow but she had too many people depending on her to let pride stand in the way. At least she'd be able to keep this from her sisters. Both were safely out of the family house and happily married now. They would never know what she was facing. Michelle glanced at a picture of her fourteen-year-old niece, Syrah, holding her new baby brother, Alex, who had his father's features and his mother's temper. Michelle smiled at the thought of Kenneth and Jasmine's new addition. He would keep their hands full. In time she would welcome news from Sean and Teresa but they were still settling into their new life together and were busy enough.

Michelle straightened an old picture of her parents on holiday in Vancouver that she kept on her desk. A small smile touched her lips. "Mum, Dad, you'd be proud. I kept them safe."

And who is to keep you safe? A cruel little voice in her head said.

"Nobody," she softly shot back, briefly glancing at the notice again, anger and a bit of sadness threatening to fill her eyes with tears. She blinked and took a deep breath. Such silly, foolish emotions. Staring at her parents' smiling faces was always a weakness. Maybe she should move the picture somewhere else. Michelle stood and placed the picture on her bookshelf, moving a crystal award for excellence in business aside to make space.

She didn't need anyone. She was strong, resilient. James had taught her that. He'd also taught her that one could survive a broken heart.

She knew her sisters worried about her being alone in their

family house, but she never felt lonely. People didn't understand that solitude could be a gift. Especially for someone like her.

Keeping secrets wasn't exhausting. It helped make her feel alive. Few things did anymore. She thought of James and the last secret he shared with her before he left her. She saw his face and remembered how much she loved him. How long she'd waited for him to come back to her, hoping for a second chance. How foolish she'd been. Her stomach twisted and her face suddenly felt hot; tears choked her throat. She had to get a hold of herself, but the strange feeling didn't leave her. She gagged and covered her mouth before rushing into the restroom afraid she might be sick.

Don't think of him. Never think of him. With trembling fingers she turned on the faucet and splashed cold water on her face, gulping in air hoping to settle her stomach. She would be fine. She was a warrior. She could handle this. *You're better than them. Stronger than them. You can fight this.* Michelle nodded at her reflection feeling better and turned to the door.

A man stood there.

A man of average height wearing a tailor made brown suit with thinning dark hair and green eyes of rage. Before she could react he grabbed her by the throat, shoving her up against the cold gray bathroom wall. She closed her eyes. Not because she was afraid, but so that she could think. Composure would be her weapon. She swallowed when she felt the cold, sharp edge of a blade pressed against her cheek but she didn't open her eyes.

"I hate you," her attacker said, spit landing on her face as he spoke. "I hate everything about you. You cost me everything. I believed you. I believed all this. Fifteen years later what do I have to show? A broken marriage, kids who won't talk to me and a failed business. You messed with my head. I can't prove it but I know it. I won't let you do it anymore. You have to be stopped."

"Yes," Michelle responded in a quiet voice. She wouldn't

panic. She would not provoke him. She would show no pain. She hadn't even been in business for fifteen years. It had only been six, but he needed someone to blame and she was his target. He was touching her so she would use that to her advantage. She could feel the anger raging within him. She covered his hand, the one he had around her throat, not to stop him, but to find a way to control him. He'd only been a client for less than a year. She remembered his hunger for help, it was too late that she recognized it as desperation. He'd owned a failed franchise, developed a candy nobody wanted and now owned a home goods store bleeding red every month. But he wouldn't listen to her suggestions, argued with experts and refused to change. She had told him a week ago that neither she nor her team could help him any longer.

She quickly searched her mind for his name. His first name started with an 'R' and ended with a 'y'. Ray? No. Roy. Her mind seized the name with satisfaction. Roy Lewis, forty-five, bright but arrogant. She'd initially felt sorry for him, but she'd learned that the most pathetic clients could be the most dangerous. It didn't surprise her that he would blame her for his failings. He couldn't face that the problem was him.

"I'm very powerful," she said, acknowledging his accusation. She opened her eyes but kept them lowered and focused on his jacket. Staring directly at him would be perceived as a threat. She knew the power of her gaze. "You were always so bright, Roy. You're one of the few people who notice it. I try to hide it well, but I should have known I couldn't fool you."

"Damn straight."

Michelle lifted her gaze to his chin. "Right now you're feeling very angry, upset, frustrated. Worried."

He shook his head and frowned. "Worried?"

"Worried that you're making things worse, that there's no

turning back. But you're wrong. You can end this now. No, I won't press charges," she said keeping her voice soft, making sure to fill his mind with only what she wanted him to believe. "You snuck into my office without anyone seeing you and no one else saw the knife except me, how clever of you, so we can pretend nothing happened. It would be my word against yours and why would I want to say anything? Why would I want to announce that I'd failed one of my clients?" He hesitated and she knew she had him. "You're going to hand the knife to me."

"I am?"

Michelle nodded and held out her free hand. "You were going to anyway. You only wanted to scare me. You did a good job."

Roy handed her the knife as if in a dream state. Michelle held the knife in her hand and finally met his gaze. She saw his eyes widen with fear. He started to release his hold around her neck, but she stopped him with her hand still around his wrist.

"No," Michelle said in the same soft soothing voice. "I won't use it. But it is tempting. What would happen if...I did attack you and say that you attacked me first? How did you get in here? Did you avoid all the cameras? Are you sure you were that clever?"

His eyes widened further and he tried to pull his hand from her grasp. "Wha...what are you?"

Michelle tightened her grip, holding his gaze. "You're not afraid of me. You're afraid of what you already know. What you don't want to face. You never wanted her anyway. Your wife was such a nag. You told me that. You told me that you married her because your mother wanted you to. That you've always done what your mother wants and you're tired of it. You love your kids but the life you have now isn't yours and you want to make your own life. You never wanted any of this. If your wife hadn't forced you to try to be like her brother you would have stayed small with your store but you were forced to expand too quickly. Now it feels like it's all too late, but it's not. You can still succeed. I can help you do that. Or you can leave it all behind and start fresh. Wouldn't you like that? To get away from all of this?"

He nodded suddenly wordless, his gaze never leaving her face.

"Then go," she said, sensing that his anger was gone. They were both safe now. "You're free."

"Free?" he echoed.

She nodded.

He blinked, ran a hand through his hair causing a few strands to stick up. "I'm sorry, I don't know what came over me."

Michelle shrugged. "It happens to the best of us. Goodbye."

"Bye," Roy said then he walked away in a semi-daze.

Michelle struggled to keep herself from sinking to the floor. Controlling him had used up more strength than she'd expected. But she'd avoided a crisis and she knew he wouldn't be back. It would all seem like a dream to him. Michelle pushed herself from the wall, straightened her shoulders and left the restroom. She put the knife in the desk drawer and closed it with satisfaction.

That's when she noticed her right hand. Something was wrong with the ring on her finger. The emerald stone was missing. Her hand trembled as she stared at the empty setting. The sight of its absence filling her with fear greater than Roy's rage. How could she have lost it? Roy had struck her hard, but had it been hard enough to dislodge and break it? An emerald wasn't the strongest of stones but it had lasted nearly ten years.

I need you, a faint deep voice whispered in her mind. Michelle brushed the words from her thoughts. They didn't mean anything and she had to focus. She couldn't become fanciful and make them mean more than they were.

The stone. The stone. She had to find the stone.

Where could she have lost it? She hurried back into the restroom and fell on her knees, her hand sweeping along the cold, hard tiles; her gaze frantically searching for the glimmer of green. She could lose anything—the office space, her home, even her business, but not this. She needed this. Please. Please. Please.

Before she could despair of ever finding it, Michelle saw the small emerald tucked under the basin.

I need you, the faint voice whispered again. His voice.

Michelle seized the emerald in her fist. If only that were true. If only James needed her. But she knew it was her imagination overreacting to a stressful event. James would never need her. She took a deep breath and opened her palm and looked at the octagon cut shape. She stared into its deep vivid hue which was not too dark or too light. It had no brown or blue undertones but a pure deep green and, to her dismay, she noticed a slight crack on the edge. That did not bode well for her. The emerald was not only a stone of romance or seeker of love and revealer of truth. It was also a stone of wisdom. A stone that had brought James into her life but hadn't helped her keep him. Was this the sign that she'd truly lost him forever? Was it something that she needed to face?

Michelle walked to her desk, pulled off the ring on her finger and set it down as shadows filtered through the large window suddenly dimming the once bright light in the room. She didn't expect that the sight of the sun disappearing behind grey clouds would shake her and when she carefully placed the emerald next to the empty ring setting, she didn't expect to cry.

CHAPTER 2

And the creature with its beady red eyes and long, sharp talons swooped down and came for her...

"Sweets, wake up. It's just a dream."

Teresa opened her eyes and looked around the dark bedroom in a daze. A sliver of moonlight seeming to dance across the floor before her; the air feeling chilled although the bed sheets felt heavy. "What?"

Sean touched her sweat soaked cheek. "Shh...you're okay."

She heard his words but her heart wouldn't stop racing. "What happened?"

He turned on the lights causing them both to squint against the hard glare, but when he spoke his voice was soft, soothing. "It was only a dream."

Teresa soon felt her heartbeat slowing as a gentle calm filled her. She looked at her husband and sighed with regret. "Did I wake you?"

He blinked, his hazel gaze intense. "No."

She couldn't stop a smile. "Liar."

He smiled in return, making all her past fears disappear. His rare smiles always had that affect on her. "Are you okay now?"

"Yes, I'm sorry."

"What happened?"

Teresa sat up and wiped the back of her hand against her forehead, her heart picking up pace again as she thought of her dream. No, it wasn't quite a dream and it wasn't a nightmare. It was something more sinister—a warning. "It was awful. I saw something dark coming. A bird with wide, dark wings and beady red eyes. I don't know what it is though but it swooped down and got her." She shivered at the thought.

Sean lay on his side, resting his head on his hand, his springy dark curls plastered on one side, and stared up at her. "Got who? One of the patients?" he asked, refering to the community clinic where he volunteered. As a former surgeon he knew few people in their struggling county could afford him and he was wealthy enough to be able to donate his time. Also, unlike some, he took his wife's visions seriously. "Us?"

Teresa shook her head. "No, Michelle."

He paused for a moment letting her words sink in. That surprised him. Teresa had never been worried about her older sister, Michelle, before. "Are you scared because she's alone at the house? The neighborhood seems safe enough and there are plenty of women living alone nowadays, but I could go by and check on her."

"It's not that." Teresa shook her head in frustration, wishing she had the words. "It's something else, but I don't know what it is. I've never really worried about her before." And the thought of the wicked dark bird loomed again in her mind, causing her throat to close in fear. Michelle was in danger. But from what? Whom? Why?

Sean touched Teresa's cheek again and she felt her fears seeping away. It still amazed her how quickly he could do that, but he had the special touch of a healer and handler, one able to touch anything without fear of breaking it, so there was magic in his fingers. She gently pushed his hand aside. "Stop that."

He feigned a look of innocence. "What?"

"I don't need to feel better and I don't want to be comforted anymore. I have to be sharp. I have to be a little afraid if I want to help her." She had to understand what she'd seen. It didn't make sense. She'd never truly felt that Michelle was in trouble before, not by anything dark. Was it loneliness? Heartache? Her sister kept so much to herself. Teresa never could tell what Michelle was thinking. Perhaps if she spoke to her friend Bertha, she could help her interpret the vision.

Sean sat up and gathered her in his arms. "Go back to sleep, we'll talk more tomorrow."

"I don't think I can sleep."

"You can," he whispered.

Teresa yawned and blinked, her eyelids feeling heavy as a slow drowsy feeling came over her. Before she completely surrendered, she realized what he was doing and pushed him away. "I said cut that out."

Sean released her and buried his face in his pillow. He moaned and mumbled something.

Teresa nudged him with her leg. "What?"

He turned to her. "I'm tired and I have a full day tomorrow. And I won't sleep if you don't sleep."

She pushed the covers away. "It's okay. I'll go to the other room."

He sighed and grabbed her wrist. "No, I'm listening."

Teresa opened her mouth then bit her lip. He looked

exhausted and there wasn't much more she could do tonight. The warning would come again if it was important. She pulled the sheets back up and slid down next to him. "Go to sleep."

"Are you okay now?"

"Yes," she said knowing only half of it was a lie.

CHAPTER 3

Michelle sat with impatience inside the hushed elegant interior of Fedor Malenkov Jewelers. It was the last place she wanted to be, but she had to fix her ring. She sent a look at her cousin BJ wondering why it was taking him so long to study her ring as he sat behind his ergonomically correct workbench, which he'd said had almost eliminated the discomfort of days hunched over his work. Clearly the new bench had given him more patience than she had. The stone needed to be fixed and then reset. What more was there?

But BJ was a man of few words and slow movement. Michelle glanced at the heavy canvas apron he wore over a dark shirt and trousers. He had beautifully sculpted ebony features that were wasted on a man who rarely smiled and preferred the company of gems, antique pins and pendants to people. She'd managed to make a discreet appointment with him after hours so that her sister Jessie wouldn't find out since she also sometimes worked at the shop. Michelle knew if BJ had questions about her broken ring, Jessie would have even more.

"Do you think you can fix it?" Michelle finally asked, no longer able to bear his silence.

He set his loupe down and sent her a brief look of reproach. "Of course I can. I'm trying to figure out what happened."

"It was an accident."

He fell silent again then said, "This may not have happened if you'd allowed me to do a cleaning and inspection twice a year. It helps prevent damage that can occur from normal wear and tear."

"I don't need a lecture right now."

"But that aside," BJ continued as if she hadn't spoken, taking no offense to her sharp tone, "this shouldn't have happened. Uncle said—"

"How long will it take to fix?"

BJ sent her a long look. "What's the rush?"

"I feel naked without it."

He sent her another long, searching look before he said, "What's going on?"

"Nothing."

"The emerald shouldn't have fallen out. That's a bad sign."

"You just told me—"

"I know what I just said, but I was only talking because I know how much you hate when I don't say anything."

She frowned, annoyed by his insight. "You were humoring me?"

He shrugged then returned his gaze to the stone. "We both know that this ring is different." He looked at her. "You're different."

She sighed. "I got angry and threw it against the wall. Okay?"

From his expression it was clear that wasn't okay. "You don't throw things."

"I did this time."

He nodded but he didn't believe her, however she knew he wasn't going to ask any more questions. At times, the fact that he wasn't the talkative type was useful to her. "Come back in a few days," he said. "Same time. Jessie won't be around. I'll buzz you in the same."

"Thanks."

"I'm good at keeping secrets." He lifted a brow. "In case you were wondering."

"I know." She stood and grabbed her handbag off the back of her chair. "It's a family trait."

MICHELLE LEFT THE SHOP, rubbing her arms, feeling suddenly chilled in spite of the warm evening, the sky fresh with the scent of rain that had yet to fall. A bad sign BJ had said. No, she wouldn't see it that way. She couldn't. If she'd told him the truth about Roy he'd understand, but then he may worry. And she didn't need that. She also couldn't tell him about the Winfields. That would truly bother him. Her story wouldn't waver. She'd gotten angry and thrown it.

And for her own piece of mind she'd relegate it to happenstance. The ring had gotten damaged after a frightening experience, that was all. There was no more to the story than that. Although stories were the life blood of the Cliftons. Her father had been full of them. He shared riveting tales and harrowing adventures that he'd carried with him from Jamaica that were always ready on his lips. He had been an older man who'd settled into family domesticity later in life. But his specialty was the stories behind metals and gems that he told. He'd worked at the jewelry store most of his life and had apprenticed BJ.

She still remembered the story he'd told her when he'd given her the emerald ring as a gift on her twentieth birthday.

"This is how he'll find you," he'd said as they sat alone in the kitchen among the sweet scent of a half eaten chocolate cake sitting in the center of the round table, while the sound of laughter from her mother and two sisters drifted from the living room where they watched TV.

Michelle looked down at the bright green gem staring up at her, settled in a dark blue velvet ring box. "Who?"

"Your soul mate."

Michelle sniffed. She'd grown beyond the tales he'd told them as children and college had given her an insight into a world she knew he would never understand. "I don't believe in soul mates."

He shrugged. "They exist whether you believe in them or not."

"If he were a true soul mate he wouldn't need this ring for me to find him."

"For him to find you," her father gently corrected.

Michelle sighed. "You know what I mean."

"You think you're so smart. And you are smart, but you're not wise. You still have a lot to learn and not every man will be comfortable with your ability."

"I can lie."

"All your life?"

"If I have to."

"No, it will weaken you. You must find someone who can handle your strength. This will also help you to channel your energy. Take your time to learn all its power."

"Why was I born this way?"

"Because you were meant to be. You are what you are. Now put the ring on and stop asking silly questions."

Michelle took the ring and slid it on her finger feeling both happy and sad at the same time, never realizing that in a year his prediction would come true.

That night, she remembered overhearing her parents in her father's workshop in the basement. She'd gone to ask him a question but had paused when she'd heard her mother scold her father for Michelle's birthday gift. "What if the others get jealous?" she'd said, her tone pointed with more clipped English tones than her father's languid Caribbean replies. Her mother's black British background was more strict and regulated than her father's.

"Jessie doesn't wear jewelry," her father said, "and I gave Teresa a bracelet for a birthday that's passed. I'm not playing favorites and my daughters know that."

"It's an expensive gift."

Michelle heard her father's chair squeak and she imagined him leaning back. "She's worth it."

"It may not work anyway," her mother said with a sigh of regret.

"It will work."

"You shouldn't have told her about a soul mate. She'll be disappointed when it doesn't happen. I don't believe in getting her hopes up. If she focuses on her studies and develops a career she can support herself and be there for her sisters."

"She needs to have a life of her own."

"We're lucky to have lived as long as we have. It was a risk to have them so late in life and they're still young. When we're gone they'll need her."

Her father's soft voice took on a hard, angry tone she'd rarely heard before. "She will not be sacrificed because we had them so late in life. We are fortunate to have had them at all."

"Most families like ours have the one child who devotes their life to the unit. Michelle doesn't need to get married. She has shown no sign of interest in what regular girls do."

"Our girls aren't regular."

Her mother fell silent a moment before she said, "Michelle even more so. I knew it when I first held her. She had eyes that were so old."

"An old soul that need not be lonely."

"She's named after my great-aunt who never married and had a wonderful life."

Michelle heard her father's chair squeak again and imagined him leaning forward. "Yes, but Teresa saw her wedding day."

"We know Teresa may marry and she dreams about many things. She—"

"No," her father said in an insistent voice. "She saw *Michelle's* wedding day."

Her mother fell silent. "More than once?"

"Yes. Four times."

"How is that even possible?"

"Many things are possible which is why I gave her the ring. There is a man out there for her and if he is a strong talent too, she will need all her resources to keep their union strong."

Her mother's voice turned to one of awe and hope. "I pray we live to meet him."

"Me too."

To Michelle's delight their wish had come true. They had been at her wedding—both loving James as much as she did—and it had been one of the most surprising and wonderful days of her life. But the ring hadn't managed to keep everything from falling apart.

CHAPTER 4

S he didn't know why she was there. Jessie Clifton glanced at the clock in the crowded Rolland Café and sighed. She'd had plans to visit the Historic Society and listen to a lecture on *Fabergé and the Russian Crafts Tradition* before she took Alex to the park. Instead she'd had to apologize to the nanny and reschedule her day because of Teresa's strange, but urgent phone call. Last night she'd been halfway up the stairs when her cell phone rang. She'd just returned from playing tennis with her friend, Wendy, and all she wanted to do was shower and change. "Would you mind if Michelle stayed at your house for a while?" Teresa asked her without preamble.

Jessie stopped walking, startled by the question. Even with a full nursery, a room for the nanny, Syrah's room and Freda, the housekeeper, plus the master bedroom they still had plenty of space. "No, but Michelle would never—"

"I'm not asking you if *she* would, I'm asking you if that would be a problem."

Jessie continued up the stairs at a slower pace, trying to

process her sister's question. "No, you know there's enough room for a football team here and I don't think Kenneth would mind."

"Good. I need you to meet me at Rolland's Café tomorrow at two."

Unfortunately, Teresa had disconnected before Jessie could ask for more details. Rolland's wasn't a real café. Its chrome booths, large windows and red cushions gave the decor the appearance of easygoing elegance but its excellent food and talented wait staff made it a pricy option for most. As the wife of a successful CEO of a software company, money was no longer a concern, but, especially since it was one of her husband's favorite places, eating there was still always a treat.

Except when it was unexpected. Jessie looked across the table at her eldest sister, Michelle, who looked just as impatient as Jessie felt. Her sister looked like the savvy business success she was, dressed in a severe dark blue suit her blunt chin length haircut emphasized her striking cheekbones giving her an elegance and class that took attention away from her plain features. Jessie had pulled her own black hair back in a ponytail and wore black sneakers to match her dark jeans and peach top with only a pair of earrings her husband had bought her and light red lipstick to offset her own unremarkable features. They made an odd pair—Michelle always looking ready to close a deal or deposit a large cheque while Jessie looked like she was headed for a run or a walk along a bike trail.

Fortunately, they were too well-known by the people in the community for anyone to care.

Michelle scrolled through something on her cell phone. "Do you know what this is about?" she asked in what others would think was a cool, neutral tone, but Jessie knew was far from it. Michelle was annoyed.

"No," Jessie said feeling her response wasn't a complete lie. "Teresa only told me to meet her here."

"I'll give her ten more minutes then I have to be somewhere else."

"She has to come from South Bank," Jessie said mentioning the neighboring county to theirs, "that's almost forty minutes away."

Michelle shot her sister a glance lacking any sympathy. "Then she should have left sooner."

Jessie felt her temper flare. "It sounded important."

"She better not be pregnant," Michelle grumbled then shook her head in regret when Jessie stared at her appalled. "That came out wrong. I mean I hope it's something that she couldn't have told us over the phone. I have something really important that I have to deal with right now."

"Something more important than your family?"

Michelle flashed a thin smile. "Still so dramatic."

"I'm not being dramatic, it's an honest question."

Michelle set down her phone. "Yes, there are some things more important than family."

Jessie held her gaze. "Like what?"

Michelle clicked her tongue in sympathy. "Sometimes new mothers can be so blind. How is Alex?"

"He's fine," Jessie said through thin lips, pricked by her sister's subtle insult."What's more important than family?"

"Survival."

She frowned. "What does that mean?"

"It's something you never have to worry about anymore."

Jessie's frown deepened. "You're not making any sense."

"No," Michelle said slowly. "I'm making perfect sense. You just don't understand what I'm saying."

Jessie felt her head begin to throb. She hated when her sister got into her superior, condescending moods. She opened her mouth to offer a cutting reply then noticed something odd about Michelle's hand. "Wait. Where's your ring?"

Michelle covered her hand, suddenly self-conscious. "I'm getting it cleaned."

Jessie looked at her with doubt. "Really? You've never gotten it cleaned before."

"I'm here. I'm here. I'm here," Teresa said, rushing over to the table with the perfect timing of a middle child who had defused many battles between her two passionate siblings. Although her features were as equally plain as the others, she had gentle eyes and a soft round face that matched her full figure.

She flopped, breathless, in a chair beside Jessie, her bracelets clinging together. She was not used to running and it showed. Aside from her heavy breathing, her bright orange peasant blouse was damp with sweat. "I'm sorry," she said between breaths. "I... got stuck...behind a tractor...and couldn't overtake it. And then I couldn't find parking..."

"It's okay," Jessie said quickly when Michelle opened her mouth. "Drink something and take your time. We're not in a rush." She hid a grin when she saw Michelle's eyes narrow.

"Thanks," Teresa grabbed the glass of water in front of her and took a long gulp before setting it back down. She took a deep breath. "I needed that."

"Why are we all here?" Michelle said ready to get down to business.

"I want you to sell the family house and come live with one of us," Teresa said.

Michelle's gaze shifted from one sister to the other. "Am I supposed to start laughing now?"

"No."

"Why would I do that?" she said after a tense silence.

"Because a monster is coming to get you."

Jessie looked at Teresa startled. "You didn't tell me that." She turned to Michelle, waving her hands. "She didn't tell me she was going to say that. I had no idea." She held up her right hand as if ready to make a vow. "I swear."

Michelle sipped her lemonade before she said with a slight grin, "I believe you."

"I'm serious," Teresa said. "I'm not making this up."

Michelle nodded. "I can deal with monsters."

"Not something like this. I saw a monster in my dream."

"Nightmares can be—"

"It wasn't a nightmare," Teresa shot back. "I saw a dark black bird with wide wings and red eyes."

"Ol' Hige," Michelle said unconcerned, referring to a witch known to shed her skin and flies about at night, sucking out people's breaths while they slept.

"No, she comes in the form of an owl or a cat."

"In Dad's story she was always an owl," Jessie said, thinking of the many folktales about the mythical creature. "I used to sleep with salt near my bed for years." It was said the witch was vulnerable to salt.

Teresa shook her head. "You're not listening to me."

Michelle rested her chin in her hand, bored. "You really expect me to uproot my life because you had a strange vision?"

Teresa nodded.

Michelle sat back and folded her arms. "Fine. Can you tell me what this monster vision means?"

Teresa sighed. "Not yet, but I'm going to talk to Bertha and—"

"You should have spoken to Bertha first." Michelle grabbed her handbag ready to leave. "Instead of wasting all of our time."

"Don't be mean," Jessie said, seeing Teresa's face fall. "She is really worried about you."

Michelle held her arms out to the side. "As you can see I'm fine." She looked at her outstretched arms and grinned. "For all you know perhaps I'm the dark bird."

Teresa frowned. "You're not a monster."

"Usually," Jessie said under her breath.

Teresa nudged her.

Michelle slid out of her seat. "When you have more perhaps I'll listen then."

"You will listen," Teresa said in a fierce tone.

"Monsters aside," Jessie said, seeing the outrage on Michelle's face. Her sister didn't like being told what to do. "Teresa has a point. Isn't the house a lot to maintain? We have plenty of space and—"

Michelle made a dismissive gesture with her hand. "I'm fine where I am."

Teresa's eyes widened and she grabbed Michelle's hand. "You're not fine. Where's your ring?"

Michelle quickly glanced around then shot her a look. She slid back into the booth and said in a harsh whisper, "Will you lower your voice?"

Teresa tugged on her sister's hand. "Where is it?"

"She's getting it cleaned," Jessie said sounding unconvinced.

Teresa looked at Michelle, her expression just as full of doubt. "I won't let you fight this alone."

Michelle snatched her hand away. "There is nothing to fight. There are no monsters."

"And the ring?"

"I'll get it back soon. Now, if we're finished—"

"Tell us what happened," Teresa said in an urgent whisper. "This is not the time for secrets."

Michelle rubbed the bridge of her nose. "There's nothing to tell. The ring—"

"What happened between you and James?"

Michelle tilted her head to the side. "I thought we were talking about monsters."

"Maybe we are."

Michelle lifted her glass then set it back down, agitated. "Why are you changing the subject?"

"Because I think it's connected. Your separation, the ring, and—"

"Are we going to order anything?" Jessie asked.

"You can," Michelle said. "I'm not staying." She lifted her lemonade and finished it in one long swallow. "I'll see you later."

"It's connected, isn't it?" Teresa said.

Jessie motioned to a waiter. "Could we get some stuffed mushrooms and another lemonade without ice?" She looked at Michelle's empty glass. "You're still thirsty, right?"

Michelle's tone hardened. "I'm not staying."

"Please tell us," Teresa said.

"Yes, another lemonade," Jessie said to the waiter who nodded then left.

"They're connected," Teresa said satisfied.

Michelle gripped the empty, cold lemonade glass to keep her hand from shaking. "You're wrong. It was a simple ordinary mistake. James and I were—are not compatible."

"Then why not get a divorce?"

"Too busy." She stood. "If that's all, I have to go."

"Michelle—"

She left.

Teresa watched her go with regret. "Maybe I shouldn't have —Ow!" Teresa said when Jessie hit her in the arm.

Jessie glared at her. "What is wrong with you? Monsters? Really?"

Teresa rubbed her arm and said in a small voice, "I didn't know how else to describe what I saw."

"And James?" Jessie gazed up at the ceiling exasperated. "Why did you have to bring James up too?" She looked at Teresa perplexed. "You know that's a sore spot."

Teresa bit her lip feeling contrite. "I know, but…how much do we know about him?"

"Why are you thinking about him all of a sudden?"

Teresa threw up her hands. "I don't know. That's the trouble. Nothing makes sense yet but he came to my mind for a reason and I can't ignore it."

The stuffed mushrooms arrived with the lemonade. Jessie reached for it while Teresa eyed one of the mushrooms. She reached for one close to her then stopped.

"What's wrong?"Jessie asked her.

Teresa frowned. "I just realized that I never touched him."

"Who?"

"James."

"You must have touched him once." Jessie took one of the mushrooms and popped it in her mouth.

Teresa shook her head. "Not in a real way. I never got a sense of him. He was always very friendly, but I never shook his hand. He always offered a hug or a kiss on the cheek."

Jessie ate another mushroom. "So what?"

Teresa set two mushrooms on her plate affectionately envying her sister's athletic build. She could have a baby, eat what she wanted and still have a killer figure. Teresa didn't have the same privilege although she was comfortable with her size. "What if he wasn't what he seemed? What if he hurt Michelle?"

Jessie stopped with a mushroom halfway to her lips. "You mean physically?"

Teresa nodded unable to say the words.

Jessie set the mushroom down and chewed the edge of her thumbnail. "I never saw—"

"You should know better than anyone that abuse can be hidden."

The sisters shared a look, knowing they were both thinking about the trauma both Jessie's husband and adopted daughter had suffered.

Jessie shook her head. "I would have hoped she would have told us."

"Perhaps she was ashamed."

"So you think that James might be coming back? That he's the monster?"

"I don't know," Teresa said dismayed. Teresa ate one of the mushrooms then said in a thoughtful voice, "I know I should have waited until I understood more, but this feels urgent. As if something is going to happen. I just have this feeling that she's in trouble."

"Nothing we can do if she won't let us help her."

"Did you ever do a reading for James?"

Jessie glanced away, scratching her chin. "You know I don't do readings for family." When Teresa didn't reply, she looked at her and faced Teresa's knowing look. She relented. "Okay, I sometimes break the rules, but I didn't for him. There didn't seem to be a need to. Mum and Dad liked him. Michelle was happy. I liked him. We all did. I truly thought they would be happy together."

"But something went wrong."

"Yes."

"If Dad were around he would know what to do."

"And you think if we figure that out we can keep Michelle safe?" Jessie said.

Teresa nodded. "Do you think Kenneth could help?"

"I don't know," Jessie said uncertain but the quiet fear in her sister's eyes gave her more boldness. "Okay, I will talk to him and see what he can do."

CHAPTER 5

Kenneth looked at his wife and laughed at what she'd just asked him to do. They sat together on the side of their bed facing the door where they had been shooting a soft stripped orange ball through the basketball hoop fixed there. The window was open but the blinds were draw against the dark night sky outside their large master bedroom where they could hear the soft rustle of a wind sweeping through the many trees surrounding the house. "You want me to do what?"

Jessie frowned at the sound of his laughter. "I want you to talk to Michelle."

"About her ex-husband," Kenneth said in a grave voice. He stood to retrieve the ball. He wore stripped pajama bottoms and an extra long red T-shirt that covered most of his scars. She knew T-shirts were still not something he felt comfortable wearing in public.

"They're not divorced yet."

He corrected himself. "Her *estranged* husband then." He sat down beside her. "Really?"

"Yes, Teresa thinks..." Jessie paused knowing it wouldn't be wise to mention the monster theory yet. "...there might have been abuse."

Kenneth's brows shot up before anger clouded his gaze, the soft basketball became a deformed mash in his tight grip. "Then it's good he disappeared."

"What if he comes back?"

His tone darkened. "I'll make sure he regrets it."

Jessie cleared her throat. She knew her husband could be dangerous when he was angry and that was not why Teresa had wanted her to approach him. She covered her hand over his as a signal to release the ball. He did. "We want to make sure first," she said, trying to reshape it. "So I think you should talk to her."

"I don't know why you think she'd talk to me when—"

Jessie turned towards the basket. "You have a way with people." She threw the ball pleased when it hit its target. "People like you for some odd reason."

He sighed.

She grinned and rested her head on his shoulder feeling him weakening. "Please."

He abruptly stood up, causing her to fall over onto the bed. "No."

Jessie sat up and clasped her hands together. "Pretty please."

Kenneth picked up the ball, shaking his head. "No. She won't talk to me."

Jessie walked over to him, resting a hand on his chest. "At least try."

He glanced down at her hand. "That's not going to work."

She slid her hand underneath his T-shirt and gently stroked his chest. "What's not going to work?"

He shook his head unable to stop a grin. "Whatever you're trying to do."

"I'm trying to get my wonderful husband to help me. Teresa had a vision," she said then shared about the monster.

Kenneth squeezed his eyes shut and groaned before he looked at her again. "You're sending me into the lion's den. You know that, right?"

Jessie nodded and grinned up at him. "Yes, but I know something else too."

"What?"

"You can handle it." She hugged him.

The sound of a baby's cry came through the monitor. When Kenneth didn't move Jessie released him and said resigned, "I'll check."

"Joyce can do it," he said referring to their live-in nanny.

"I'll be right back."

Moments later she returned and closed the window before she slid in bed beside him.

"Everything okay?" Kenneth asked.

"Yes."

"Good." He turned off the lights.

Jessie was silent a moment before she said, "When are you going to hold him?"

She felt him shift beside her. "One day."

"When? When he's seventeen?"

"That sounds about right."

She playfully hit him in the chest. "Kenneth, you won't break him."

He ran a hand down his face. "I know."

"He's six months already."

"I know that too. At least he's sleeping through the nights more."

"Kenneth—"

"Jasmine," he said in a quiet voice, using her given name. He was the only one she allowed to use it. "Be patient with me."

She sighed. "Goodnight."

Kenneth closed his eyes knowing he'd been given another reprieve. He knew it was an irrational fear but he hadn't managed to conquer it. But until he did he couldn't risk being near his son. Too much was at stake. He needed his wife to be patient with him. He hadn't stood by and done nothing. He'd provided her with all the help she needed, let her know that she didn't need to go back to work if she didn't want to yet; he'd surprised her with gifts to let her know how much he cared and so far she had been understanding and patient. But everyday judgment day loomed because he knew that one day her patience would run out.

CHAPTER 6

*P*oor *Kenneth*, Michelle thought as she watched her brother-in-law make his way to their table in the coffee shop with two cups in his hand. The moment she had gotten a text from him to meet for drinks she knew he'd been sent by her sister. But no one would ever suspect it. Kenneth looked like a man in charge of the world as he smiled at the barista, making her blush; made a shy clerk giggle, another swoon and an older woman beam with delight and all within the five minutes he'd entered the coffee shop.

But he'd always been that way, even as a child. She could remember how much her parents had loved him and how much her sister Jessie had once resented him for it. Michelle laughed in remembrance still amazed by how much had changed.

Kenneth set a steaming cup down in front of her and smiled. "Thanks for meeting me."

Up close his impact was even more impressive. Michelle hated to admit it, but there were times he was unnervingly hand-some. He was a large man with cinnamon skin, a hundred watt smile and incredible charm. Sometimes too much so. She could tell by his intense, yet tender, gaze that he had been sent on a mission by her sister to talk to her, but there was no guile or pretense. She could tell he was genuinely concerned.

"Okay, spill it," Michelle said ready to put the poor man out of his misery. "Ask me what Jessie won't."

"Did James ever hurt you?"

She hesitated, she hadn't expected that question. She took a long sip of her coffee then carefully set the cup down. "No."

"Are you sure?"

"Of course I'm sure."

Kenneth leaned forward his beautiful, brown eyes holding her still. "If he made you think it was your fault…"

"He didn't hurt me." *Not on purpose and not like that. Never like that.* But she wouldn't know how to explain it. And talking about him made her miss him and she hated missing something. *Don't think about him! It's over.* When Kenneth's keen gaze didn't move from her face she sighed. "I'm not lying."

"You hesitated."

"Because you surprised me."

"You don't surprise easily."

Michelle inwardly groaned. He could be as perceptive and annoying as BJ. "You can tell my sister that I'm all right. I've always been all right and I will be all right in the future. James never laid a hand on me, he never verbally abused me. Our marriage just fell apart."

Kenneth nodded. "Okay. Why?"

Michelle started to grin. "I've kept that secret for this long. What makes you think I'd change my mind?"

He shrugged. "I can be persuasive."

"Use your charms on someone else."

"Jasmine told me about the monster."

"Without laughing?"

Kenneth held her gaze. "I, for one, know that monsters are real."

Michelle immediately felt contrite. His history had been a bad one and she didn't want to make light of his concern. Kenneth came from a family of men who used their fists and objects when angry and Kenneth had both the internal and external scars to prove the damage they had caused. "I know. And I understand that Teresa's really worried, but I don't know how else to say it. I'm fine."

Kenneth nodded again and glanced down at his drink.

"How's being a new father?"

He quickly looked up, his expression vulnerable before a handsome, blinding smile filled his face. "Great."

"You're lying."

His gaze darkened. "No, I'm not. I love my kids."She held his gaze and his smile turned into a ruthless one. "I can tell you're itching for a fight, but do you really want to take me on? I can be brutal."

"So can I."

He shook his head, his low voice a warning. "Not enough."

Michelle lowered her gaze, knowing he was right. She did want to fight and she would lose against him. She briefly thought of asking him to help her with her fight against the Winfields. Perhaps he could help her with a strategy. He was rich, powerful, and he had connections. But he was still rebuilding his reputation from the scandal nearly three years ago and he and Jessie had been through enough. She didn't want the Winfields targeting them. Plus, if Jessie truly knew her situation she and Teresa would worry about her more.

She felt a soft squeeze on her shoulder and looked up into Kenneth's piercing gaze. "You know how to reach me if you need anything."

"Yes, of course. I'm sorry for...it's work. It's been stressful."

He winked. "Holidays were created for a reason."

She couldn't stop a smile, annoyed that he'd made her feel better if only for a moment. "I'll remember that."

"Remember this too. You're not alone."

I need you.

Michelle shoved open the front door to her house with extra force and hurried inside. Behind her a child screamed in delight down the street as its parent pushed their tricycle and she smelled someone's freshly cut lawn and new mulch. She slammed the door closed. There was that voice again. *His* voice. But it couldn't be. It seemed urgent. Stronger now. Why? Why was her mind playing tricks on her? Why was she thinking of him? She didn't want to think of him. And he didn't need her. Nobody needed her. Not like that.

Michelle set her keys and bag in the foyer and walked into the kitchen to see what she could grab for dinner. She opened her refrigerator and looked at the carton of leftovers from various restaurant takeouts. Hmm. It was an embarrassing collection of riches. What would it be tonight? Indian, Chinese, Ethiopian, Jamaican? Ah, yes she was in the mood for some red beans and rice and a little vegetable roti. She selected the black carton, dumped it on a plate and popped it in the microwave.

Later, she sat in front of her TV eating her dinner and laughing at a funny Swedish film spoofing crime dramas. She finished her dinner then stretched out on the couch feeling better. More like herself. The meeting with Kenneth had unnerved her more than it should have. And then that voice.

Hearing that silly voice again was Teresa's fault.

A monster. She knew about the monster. How could her sister know about that?

Michelle shook her head trying to rein in her thoughts. She'd been thinking about James since the letter revoking her lease had arrived. Perhaps her sister had somehow tuned into her fears. Would he be coming back? Michelle's heart picked up speed at the thought, not from fear but expectation. It then settled. No, no he wouldn't come back. There was no reason for him to return. She'd given up hoping years ago. Had it been nearly three years? More?

It didn't matter. She had moved on and she needed to show her sisters how much. She looked at her bare finger where her ring used to be. She rubbed the back of her hand, her palm feeling hot. She didn't only feel naked without it but vulnerable.

Was he behind the letter she'd received? Why hadn't he shown himself?

A monster.

A monster was coming.

James was coming back; she could somehow sense it. She would face it. But no one could know the truth. No one must ever know...

CHAPTER 7

A magician.

That was how Michelle stared at him when BJ handed her the fixed emerald ring. As if he'd worked magic. He liked the expression.

"It's a miracle," she said in awe. There were few things that awed her. "It looks perfect. As if nothing happened."

BJ nodded pretending to look humble. He knew he'd done an amazing job. "Good."

Michelle slipped the ring on her finger and BJ watched an expression of calm come over her features. He wanted to ask her again if something was wrong, but he knew that wasn't necessary. He knew something was going on with her and he also knew she wouldn't tell him about it.

"Thanks. How much was it again?"

BJ lowered his head, pretending not to hear her.

"I know we're family, but I still want to—"

"You can pay me with a clue."

"A clue?"

He met her gaze. "About what's going on with you."

Michelle's eyes flashed. "Did Teresa tell you about the monster too?"

He frowned. "Monster?"

She shook her head embarrassed. Now she was getting paranoid. "Never mind. I'm...I'm sorry. It's been a stressful week at work. Truly. And forget about payment I'll treat you to dinner. Will next Friday suit you?"

"That would be fine."

BJ watched Michelle leave the shop looking as if she had everything under control. No outsider could tell that anything was wrong by her confident walk and stylish clothes. He sighed feeling guilty. He probably shouldn't have done what he did, but he'd been curious. Two days ago he'd given the emerald to Jessie to do a reading without letting her know where or who he'd gotten it from. He hadn't been sure she could tell him much, but he'd thought it was worth a try. Outside of its setting, he didn't think that Jessie would recognize it since they saw many different stones in their line of work, plus some people still came to her for private readings.

Jessie sat next to his workbench and held the stone in her palm. "It's a lovely color and—"

"I know all the properties; I want to know more about the owner."

She frowned. "Why?" She paused. "Are you interested in this woman?"

"How do you know it belongs to a woman?" When Jessie sent him a look he realized he'd insulted her ability and half feared she'd be able to figure out its true owner. "No," he said quickly. "Not in that way. Just curious. Can you...see who owns it?"

"No, I can only sense feelings."

He breathed a sigh of relief.

"I don't usually work this way, but...for a cousin." She playfully nudged him in the side and offered a smile. "I'll make an exception." She sat back and centered herself. "Well, it's definitely a love stone. This stone is strong with the hearts of two, but..."

"But what?"

Jessie quickly set the stone down and rubbed her hands together as if it had burned her. "It's a painful love. I'm not sure it will ever be healed. The owner is truly heartbroken and in pain. Very sad."

He had been afraid of that. But he'd suspected. He knew Michelle kept things close but there had been a cold, defensive look in her gaze when she'd come to him. The gaze of a wounded animal ready to lash out at anyone trying to come too close. She'd only looked that way once before, when James first disappeared. Or left her. Or she'd kicked him out. No one really knew what had happened just that her husband was gone and she moved back into the family home. BJ wasn't close enough to do much more than speculate and his mother had warned him not to meddle, not that he would, but he felt for her. Michelle had always been nice to him. She was far from being a warm, cuddly woman—not as playful as Jessie or as comforting as Teresa—but he knew he could depend on her and whenever he had a question regarding the business she was ready to offer assistance. He wanted to do whatever little he could to help her now. "But the emerald is also a stone of healing, right?"

"True," Jessie said slowly, cautiously. "But somehow there seems to be a block." She shrugged. "Maybe I'm wrong. Perhaps the woman needs to pair the stone with something else for a better balance." She then gave him ideas for a possible necklace or ring design. BJ nodded and pretended to listen, wondering if there would ever come a day when he was forced to tell her who the stone truly belonged to.

CHAPTER 8

S he didn't like being ignored.

And she'd been ignored for an entire week.

Michelle stood in front of her office window trying to come up with a strategy for her next attack. She'd tried to be civil, but Martha hadn't replied to her messages or emails. Michelle stared out at a lost purple balloon floating up to the clear blue sky and imagined the crying child who would miss it. At six she'd had that happen to her at a fair. A kind cartoon character had handed her the smiley faced balloon, and not being used to attention from strangers, she'd cherished and wanted to keep it forever. Although her father had fastened it around her wrist, he'd been distracted because little Jessie wouldn't keep still and escaped from her push chair to run, so the knot he tied loosened and too late Michelle's cherished bright yellow balloon floated to the sky. She'd cried all the way home, not caring how her parents told her they would get her another one. She knew it wouldn't be the same. She felt the helpless pain of loss.

But she wouldn't cry now. She would fight.

If Martha wouldn't reply then she'd go one step further.

Michelle pulled out her appointment book and saw the number she had never thought she'd call again. She hesitated then sat down behind her desk. It was the only way.

The phone connected on the first ring. "I was waiting for this moment," Martha said.

Surprised by hearing the sudden voice from the past, Michelle absently opened her upper desk drawer. Roy's knife winked up at her. She quickly closed it. "I'm sorry?"

"I wondered how long it would take for you to call me. When did you get the notice?"

"Last week."

"You've become more patient."

"You won't return my calls. I left you messages and emails."

"But you took your time calling me at this number."

Because I didn't want to speak to you. She'd wanted to keep it professional—distance. Calling Martha's personal line made the exchange something more.

"Meet me this Saturday. I'll send your assistant the details."

"You can talk to me over the phone. Why should I meet with you?"

"If you want to save your business, you won't ask questions, you'll do as I say." She disconnected.

Michelle sighed. Martha Winfield was too used to getting her own way. They'd won this round, but just as she'd suspected they had something up their sleeves. Why did she want to see her? What did they really want? Michelle knew the only way to answer her questions was to do as she asked—for now. She wouldn't dance to their tune for long.

Michelle pounded her fist on the desk and swore. She had to learn not to hate her. But the jealousy was still there. Michelle thought of Martha and sighed with regret. Now she had to face the woman who James really loved. The only woman he trusted without hesitation. Not his wife, his grandmother. The one woman who could be by his side, hold his heart and keep him. Not because he was a 'momma's boy' that was too simplistic a term.

No, it was because she'd never captured his heart. He hadn't loved her that way. She hadn't been strong enough to persuade his heart to be hers. She was the failure. It had been her secret fear when she'd first met him. That what they had was all too good to be true.

This wonderful, smart, handsome, funny man had tried to love her, but in the end hadn't. That was the true sting. Not the ultimate rejection but the fact that it had all been built on a lie. She'd loved him more than he'd loved her.

She regretted letting herself believe in a fairy tale. She hadn't imagined a happily-ever-after but she had imagined commitment and devotion for life. At least her sisters had managed what she'd failed to do. She'd make sure no one ever knew the truth. How much she'd failed at something she'd worked so hard to attain.

But at least now she could put the past to rest.

Martha set down the phone and looked across her expansive hotel suite at the expectant face of one of her three sons. At fifty-five he looked a decade younger with the a heavy set build that most people mistook for overindulgence. But he was a man with a sharp mind and regulated habits. Those habits made her feel comfortable that the family business was in good hands. He was the only one she trusted to help her. "It's done."

His brows shot up in surprise. "She'll come?"

"I told you she would."

He sighed. "I don't know why we couldn't just ask her to help—"

Martha shook her head, cutting off his words. "After the way this family has treated her I doubt she'd want to do us any favors."

"But for James's sake."

Martha held up her hand touched by his affection for his nephew. "Your only job is to make sure your siblings don't find out about this."

"I won't tell them. But are you certain this is the only way?"

"We've run out of options," Martha said with grim finality. "It has to work."

CHAPTER 9

Teresa waited patiently as she sat in Bertha Walker's living room among a colorful assortment of plants, glass jars and quilted print pillows. She clasped her hands together as she waited for her friend and mentor to interpret her vision.

Bertha looked at Teresa, briefly touched the large purple turban on her head, which seemed to give her small frame the height that it needed, then said, "Your sister is going on a journey and you have to let her go."

Teresa blinked at the older woman. That was it? Bertha was known in the Jamaican immigrant community as a woman who possessed wisdom and foresight. After telling her the detail of her dream, Teresa had expected something else—something more profound. Teresa cleared her throat, wondering if she'd misunderstood her. Did she mean a spiritual journey of some sort? "Let her go where? Is she in danger? Is she in trouble? Why would she need to travel?"

"Those questions will be answered when she returns."

Teresa frowned. "Travel from where? It's not like you to speak in riddles."

Bertha shrugged, hearing the frustration in her young friend's voice but taking no notice. She'd lived long enough to know to accept life's ups and downs. "I'm saying there's nothing you can do, but be here for Michelle when she returns. And she may not return alone. When that happens you come to me."

Teresa leaned forward eager for more guidance and insight. "James...does it have anything to do with him?"

"The monster?"

Teresa nodded.

Bertha pursed her lips, a flash of annoyance crossing her face. "Was I not at your sister's wedding?"

"Yes."

"Do you think I would have stayed silent if I thought James was dangerous to her?"

Teresa lowered her head properly chastised. Of course Bertha had been at the wedding. How could she have forgotten that? She had met James. But something still bothered her.

"Did you ever shake his hand?"

Bertha sighed. "You are a tenacious one."

"The last time I saw Michelle she wasn't wearing her ring. She said she was getting it fixed. She's never been without it before. I know I might be chasing shadows, but since Michelle hasn't told me anything, I've started making up stories."

Bertha paused and closed her eyes. "There's a third presence." She opened her eyes and stared at her. "A dark presence they must both face if they want to ever be together again. That's all I can tell you." When Teresa opened her mouth Bertha shook her head. "You are to do nothing but wait and give her space to come to you when she needs to."

"What if she never does?"

Bertha flashed a knowing grin. "She will. It's time for her and James to heal the wounds of the past."

THE PAST

CHAPTER 10

ALMOST SEVEN YEARS AGO…

The man did a double take.

It was the first time that had happened to Michelle in all her twenty-one years. She glanced behind her to make sure the man had been staring at her. She may have been mistaken. The 400-room castle tucked among a rolling English hillside was undoubtedly awe inspiring at every turn from grand state apartments to private rooms filled with ornate wood carvings and painted ceilings. So it was understandable that there must be some aspect of the grand hall behind her that had caught the man's attention.

Michelle looked up at the large window behind her. Aside from an astounding view of the gardens below, which he couldn't see from where he was standing, there was only the blue sky dotted with white clouds.

Michelle turned back to the man.

Their eyes met. His a deep, magnificent brown that clung to hers like a shared secret. Her heart picked up speed. It wasn't a mistake. He was staring at *her*. Nothing else. Nobody else. Only her.

She absently remembered seeing him come into the grand hall with his head held down instead of looking up at the opulent surroundings. She'd noticed the tall black man at the beginning of the tour because he looked bored. The kind of man who could look at a glorious sunset and yawn. That kind of indifference surprised her. He had a dark, broodingly handsome air about him. He seemed too old to be a college student like her and too young to be with the traveling seniors who were part of another tour group. She noticed the older, finely dressed, attractive woman by his side as well as the older man, (he was not as old as the woman, in his forties perhaps), also finely dressed with average features. He seemed to be more interested in what the tour guide, an animated young woman with big teeth, said than the actual surroundings.

Both people didn't seem to suit him. Like the castle, the man had an ancient proud air—the profile of a king, the gait of a warrior. So when the tour took them to the grand hall Michelle glanced at him curious to see his response. Would his lip curl in disdain? His eyes squint with disinterest? Had he been forced to come? But he'd disappointed her by keeping his gaze on the ground until he abruptly glanced up at her with the same disinterested gaze he'd had with everything else before he turned away. But then miraculously, amazingly, he had turned to look at her again. It was a strange and rare thing to experience.

People rarely looked at her once, let alone twice. Especially men. She was well aware of her unremarkably plain features. Everyone knew the Clifton sisters lacked any spark of beauty. They weren't even handsome, just plain, 'plain as dishwater' one aunt liked to say, and after facing that rather cruel truth, she'd accepted it and knew she would use her intellect to get what she wanted.

In time, someone would see past her dull outer shell to the

woman within but until that happened she would travel, dress in the best clothes she could buy, learn new things and enjoy life. Which was why this summer abroad in England had been so exciting, but now this stranger—this annoyingly handsome stranger—had looked at her twice. Maybe it was because she'd been looking at him and he'd sensed it. Michelle felt her cheeks burn with embarrassment. It wasn't like her to be curious about someone like this. She wouldn't look at him again. It had been foolish of her to follow him with her eyes in the first place. Like a teenager with a crush.

She glanced at the large dining table teeming with history, then up at the candelabra above it, resisting the urge to steal another glance at him. She was certain he'd looked away, but she didn't want to take the risk. Yes, it was all just a moment. It was silly of her to think it could have been more. Only certain woman experienced the power of entering a room and having all eyes turn to them then stop and gaze in awe and wonder. Once, as a child, she had allowed herself to dream that, but then, over time became more sensible with the help of her mother. "No use wishing for things to be what they are not," she said in her clipped English tones. "Best to make use of what you have. That's the key to a woman's power."

Power. That was another problem. She had a tad too much of it. Of all the Clifton sisters hers was the most intimidating. No one feared Jessie and her ability to read stones. It was harmless and, yes, most people thought that Teresa was odd with her ability to read energy and heal with herbs. But again...harmless. Eccentric. Different.

But if anyone truly knew what Michelle could do they would be frightened. Plain faced and with frightening abilities—what an unfortunate mixture. At ten years old, she'd even overheard her parents discussing her fate while her mother tended her garden.

"She will suffer the most, poor thing," her father had said.

Her mother pulled out a weed and set it to the side. "She doesn't have to know."

"But she will find out eventually. It's best that we tell her now so that she doesn't make any mistakes."

"Marrying will be difficult. Men will use her if they know." She sighed. "I don't think she'll marry or should. Most of her type don't. Few men can handle it. Fortunately, she won't be alone. Her sisters will always be there for her and she will be there for them."

"She will be fine and she will marry."

Her mother grabbed another weed. "That's the problem with you you're always so optimistic."

"Worry is misuse of the imagination."

Michelle came around the corner. "Is there something wrong with me?"

"No, my dear," her father said with a wide grin. "You're perfect as you are."

But her father always liked to say things like that. She'd learned early not to believe him. Although she loved him he couldn't always be trusted. He lived in the clouds where she preferred her feet firmly on land. As did her mother.

Michelle let her gaze slide towards the stranger's direction. Curiosity winning over caution. The man was gone. It had been a silly, fleeting moment. She glanced down at herself wondering what could have warranted the second glance. Wishing, just a little, that he had come over and said something to her. Anything. Even something banal. Something that would have given her the chance to hold his gaze, his interest, just a little while longer. Because in that brief moment she'd seen something beautiful and familiar in his eyes that felt like home.

CHAPTER 11

James stumbled out of the grand hall into the dark hallway, gripping his chest. Not sure he could breathe. Not sure he could remain standing for much longer, but he had to. He had to recover. He would not collapse. If he did his mother wouldn't let him out again. He'd be stuck in his chair and in the some vast, over adorned room again. *I knew this trip to England would be too much for you,* she would say. *We should have gone to the islands.* This had been his chance to prove that he was better and strong enough to be on his own, but now that was being threatened. By a woman.

His assistant, Graham Hicks, rushed up to him, taking his hand. "I knew this would be too much for you."

"I'm fine. I...I just need to catch my breath."

"Climbing all those stairs. If your mother—"

"I just...need...some air." He tugged on his collar. His skin feeling prickly, the hallway beginning to spin. No he couldn't' collapse, not here. Please not here. Not when he'd come so far. He stumbled forward. He just needed some air.

"Is he all right?"

James had never heard that voice before, but somehow he knew who it belonged to. It belonged to her. The woman wearing a pair of dark jeans and a black jacket with a proud stance and silver earrings.

"Yes, he's fine," Graham said in a voice that made it clear he didn't want or need assistance. But the woman didn't seem to care because suddenly James felt her long, cool fingers on his forearm and in a low voice she said, "Of course he's fine. He's very strong. He's always been strong. And right now his breathing is calm, his heart is steady and he is perfectly fine."

And her words had the power of a spell being cast. Soon the hallway stopped spinning, his heart beat steadied as did his breathing, but, most strange of all, were his limbs. They felt weightless, his back and spine feeling straight when for weeks he'd been a little hunched over making him feel years older than his actual age. He felt as if he could run, jump, fly. Just by the touch of her hand and her words. He spun around to her, desperate to face her. "What are you?" The moment he said the words he knew he'd said the wrong thing. Something came over her features and she took a step back.

"Excuse me." She walked past them.

James reached for her but she moved too quickly. "No, wait. I'm sorry. I didn't mean—"

"There you are," his mother said hurrying towards him, her heels clicking against the floor. "What were you thinking coming up here? You look flushed. You've been overexerting yourself."

"No, I'm fine," James said, watching the woman disappear into the crowd. "I have to go."

"It's time we go back to the flat."

"Not yet. There's something I have to do."

"The doctor said—"

He didn't care. He pushed past his mother and headed for

where the woman had disappeared. She looked as if she was headed towards the gardens. He couldn't lose her. He just needed a name, something. He hurried down the stairs.

Graham chased after him. "What are you doing?"

"I have to find her."

"Who?"

"The woman who helped me. The American." At least he knew that much about her, although her US accent also had another cadence he couldn't quite place.

Graham grabbed his arm, forcing him to stop and face him. "I really think you need to take a seat. She didn't do anything."

James yanked his arm free. "What do you mean? You were there when she healed me. The words she said."

"I don't remember her saying anything." His expression of concern grew. "I think—"

James looked past him through to the exit and saw the sun glint against her earring. He pointed. "There she is!" She was outside in the garden. If he ran he could reach her. But he hadn't run in such a long time that only after a few steps his chest hurt, his legs ached. She was moving too quickly, he wasn't going to reach her. He was never going to see her again. He couldn't let that happen. He used whatever fuel he had left and by the time he reached her he had no breath left. He fell on his knees before her, taking her hand in his as a silent form of apology and stared up at her hoping his eyes could say what his body wouldn't let him.

"I'm sorry about this," Graham said to her. "He's never been like this before. He's not all there but he's harmless."

Graham's words angered him. His body may betray him, but never his mind. Not yet at least. "I didn't...mean...the words. I want...thank—"

The woman knelt down in front of him and up close he saw

how young she was, although how she carried herself seemed much older. She pressed a cool finger over his lips and he felt his body craving more of her touch. "Shhh...let your mind calm or the words won't come. But I know what they are and you're welcome. You have nothing to worry about. This weakness won't last because you're stronger than it is." She smiled then began to stand. But he stopped her, lightly tightening his grip on her hand and he saw a spark of fear in her eyes, but he couldn't let go.

"You're scaring her," Graham warned in a low voice.

God he didn't mean to. He didn't mean to scare anyone, but he just didn't have the words. He didn't have the manners of others. He felt a biting pinch on the back of the neck. "That's enough of that," his mother said. "Let's go." She addressed the young woman. "I'm sorry about this."

James inwardly screamed. He didn't want the woman to think he was crazy or not quite right in the head. He tried to meet her gaze, hoping she'd understand, but she looked at his mother and his heart fell. He shouldn't have run after her. At least she would have thought he was normal then.

"No need to apologize," she said, then surprised everyone, most of all him, by taking his hand. "We know each other. I didn't recognize him at first."

"James?" his mother said as he scrambled to his feet. "You know this woman?"

Yes, his heart cried, giving him the strength to stand tall. Yes, he'd been waiting for her his entire life and now she was here. She understood.

The woman looped her arm through his. "Could you give us a moment, please?"

"Yes, they can," James said, answering for them then turned so that they could head deeper into the garden along the pristine path of begonias and poppies. He tilted his face to the summer sun, listening to the sound of her footsteps beside him as they crunched along the gravel path, then become a hush as the path turned into a grass carpet.

"It's a lovely day, isn't it? I think so," she said, easily turning a statement into a question then back into a statement again. "And you're walking so quickly and steadily, your breathing is easy and you're not worried about anything."

He felt it. The breathless feeling ebbing away, the worry, the fear becoming a distant memory. He felt her hand on his arm. His mother had chided him for not wearing a jacket and now he was glad that he hadn't or he would have missed this chance to feel her warm hand against his skin. Her hand. No one had touched him with such command yet tenderness. His mother's touch was always tinged with possession and fear; his assistant with duty but this stranger's touch was like nothing else. No, he was wrong, she wasn't a stranger. He'd been waiting for her all his life. He focused and let her name whisper into his thoughts. The name that had been on the edge of his awareness since he was a child: Michelle. He sighed satisfied. Her name suited her. "You have a beautiful name."

She turned sharply to him, alarmed. He wasn't surprised. He'd been told once that his voice could have that affect on people. "How would you know that?"

"What?"

"I haven't told you my name yet."

That's right, she hadn't. "I-I must have overheard it."

"What do you think my name is?"

Damn, he was caught. He could be wrong. She could be named something else. He shook his head. "Never mind."

"My name's Michelle."

The tightness in his chest eased a little. He'd been right. He took a deep breath and gazed up at the sky. "I'm not crazy."

She stiffened. He'd frightened her again and hadn't meant to. "James. My name is James."

He could still feel the tension in her. He turned to her, hoping that his eyes could express what words couldn't. But when his gaze met hers the shocking awareness that had first gripped him seized him again. She wasn't afraid. She was...what was that expression on her face? What made her brown eyes shine like that? What made her eyebrows lift in surprise? "You're not afraid?"

"No, but when you were on your knees I felt as if I knew you." She shook her head. "But I know I don't."

"Do you believe in fate?"

"No."

"I do."

"James," his mother called to him. "It's time to go."

He ignored her. "And we were meant to meet. There's...so much I want to say."

"James!"

He briefly closed his eyes. Must she call him as if he were a child or her pet? "Your number, please," he said.

Michelle shook her head offering a sad smile. "I thought you believed in fate. If we're meant to meet again, we will. Remember, you're strong."

Panic gripped his heart. No, this wasn't how it was supposed to end. Not when he'd just found her. He pulled out his wallet and held out his card. "Here's my number. Call me any—"

She shook her head again. "I really don't think—"

"Please."

She quickly let his arm go and rejoined the tour group, leaving him feeling lost; his heart heavy. He let the card float to the ground. She'd lied or perhaps he'd lied to himself. But he could no longer deny it: She had been afraid of him.

Michelle returned inside the main building, pressing her hands against her burning cheeks. She bumped into a couple posing for a picture and apologized before heading aimlessly through one of the large rooms. What had come over her? Why had she taken his hand? And why had she panicked when he'd asked for her number? She'd gotten close to something wonderful —a possibility, a hope—and she'd run from it. She knew there was nothing wrong with him, despite the way the older woman and the other man treated him.

His voice was low and gravelly, not unpleasant but not soothing either. It was harsh, as if a mountain had spoken. A beautiful, majestic mountain. She loved mountains. Why hadn't she given him her number? There was no harm in giving it to him. He may not have called her anyway.

But if he had...that was her true fear.

What are you? His words still echoed in her thoughts. Not 'who' but 'what'? And his searching brown gaze had sought an answer she couldn't give. She shouldn't have touched him; she shouldn't have spoken words to try to influence him. What if he thought she'd casted a spell? She hadn't. She wasn't a witch. None of them were. What an inadequate word to describe her, but she wished she could have given him an answer. Why had she done what she had? Why had she taken his hand and pretended to know him if she was only going to run away?

But she couldn't go back because something strange had come over her. It wasn't only a feeling as if she'd known him before, but when he'd been on his knees looking up at her, she'd been transported to another place. Another time. The castle garden had fallen away replaced with a palace in ancient Ghana and she was a queen. He knelt before her pledging his heart and life. And she loved him. But although she knew it wasn't her life and it wasn't her memory the emotions felt real.

Michelle shook the memory from her mind. It was madness. She couldn't face him again and now she'd never know why he'd looked at her twice.

You were not brought up to be a coward, she could hear her mother say. Michelle glanced down at her ring and her father's words came to her mind. She didn't have to be afraid. There was someone out there who wouldn't be afraid of her gift.

Michelle raced back into the expansive garden hoping he was still there since only a couple minutes had passed, but he was gone. She searched but there was no sight of him. Her heart fell.

It was her fault for letting him go. She turned to head towards the tour bus then stopped when she saw something white skating along the gravel path. She walked over to it and picked it up. It was a business card. *His* business card. She gripped it in her hand with a smile. Perhaps she had been given another chance after all.

CHAPTER 12

Joanna had that look. That 'you're full of bullshit' look. He hated that look.

Graham sighed as he poured himself a whiskey. He took a long swallow before he set the glass down. She could drive a man to drink and had driven him to do so on a number of occasions. But she paid him enough for it though he was careful enough not to get wasted. She wasn't worth the headache. She'd been quiet on the drive back from the castle to the Kensington flat the Winfield's owned when they were in London. He knew she was upset but always waited for her to speak first. She sat in the sitting room with her legs crossed at the ankles and her gaze fixed on him.

"Do you like this job?"

He hated that question too. She always used it when she threatened to fire him. But she wouldn't. She needed him too much. "Yes, ma'am."

"Then why are you doing such a poor job of it?"

She was nervous, anxious and she needed a whipping boy. She knew what this trip meant. That her son was getting stronger, that one day he might not need her anymore. That's why Graham was around: to make sure James stayed in line. The incident at the castle had been unfortunate, but he didn't plan to see it repeated anytime soon. "It won't happen again."

Joanna sighed. "I knew letting him have his way would be a disaster."

"Not a complete disaster. He reunited with a friend."

She fixed him with another 'bullshit' look. "Did you believe that?"

"The woman seemed harmless."

"That's not the point. What if she hadn't been? What would you have done then?"

"Ma'am—"

"Do I need to remind you of your past?"

He bowed his head. *Do I need to remind you that I know all about your son?*

"Don't disappoint me again." She stood and left the room.

Graham poured another glass of whiskey and toasted the door before downing the contents.

He'd made an error at the castle. He hadn't been paying attention and he'd gotten caught. It was his job not to get caught. That was his specialty. As a Chicago cop, he hadn't gotten caught with prostitutes or the occasional missing evidence bag. As a husband, he hadn't gotten caught with the lady who delivered the dry cleaning. His marriage had broken up for other reasons too boring to list. Meeting Joanna had changed his life. He'd been one of the first officers at the scene of her nine-year-old son's accident. She'd been traumatized and scared. She'd turned to him and he'd made it his goal to comfort her.

It had turned into a profitable move when she hired him to look after James, who she said was 'accident prone'. People laughed at Graham being a glorified babysitter but when he gave them a round figure of what he earned they stopped laughing. And if that wasn't enough, a quick punch to the jaw usually did it.

Being around the Winfields showed him a side of life he'd never imagined. The travel, the food, the surroundings were a far cry from his Southside upbringing. Graham looked at the solid white gold diamond ring on his pinkie. It had been a gift from Joanna for his fifth year anniversary. He hadn't thought he'd last more than a year looking after James. But the job came easy. James's father was rarely around, so Graham took his place, not quite as a father figure—Joanna would not have allowed that—but as another man to emulate. A man who knew his place. Joanna liked her men that way, which is probably why her husband stayed gone. She hadn't even taken on his surname, preferring to be referred to as Ms. Winfield, and neither had her son.

As a boy James wasn't spoiled but he wasn't normal either. Now at twenty-five he was trying to create his own life. Joanna wouldn't like that.

And Graham liked his job too much to like it either, but he had to be careful to not let either side know what he was up to.

He had to keep Joanna happy and James would have to re-learn his place in the family.

"I don't know how he could have let it happen. It was absolutely awful."

Joanna sat in the living room with her sister-in-law, Angela, a tray of tea and biscuits on the table between them. It had been hours since the castle incident but she was still upset and had called Angela to cheer her up.

"You still haven't told me what happened," Angela said, eying a biscuit she wouldn't dare touch. She sighed. Tea and biscuits. Why did it always have to be tea and biscuits? Or tea and sandwiches? Just once couldn't it be wine and cheese? Angela looked at the chocolate covered biscuit again. She was trying to cut back on sweets. She wanted to maintain her slender frame although she knew she could easily burn the calories off at the club later, but she still wished Joanna had more of an imagination.

"It was something awful, dreadful."

Angela blinked slowly. "Yes, you've said that." When Joanna didn't expand she said, "Am I supposed to guess or will you fill in the blanks?"

Joanna rubbed her forehead. "I'm sorry. I'm still so shaken. It could have been a disaster. I don't know how to put it into words."

"Beating about the bush doesn't make it any clearer I'm afraid."

"James met a woman."

Angela sipped her tea. It could use more sugar but she was cutting back on that too. "James doesn't know any women. I'm not even sure he likes them."

"She said she knew him."

Angela looked at the sugar bowl. Would one more sugar lump be so bad? Joanna liked her tea blends so bitter and since it was the only thing to drink... She reached for the tongs. "Do you believe her?"

"No, but what was worse was that he lied to me." Joanna tapped her chest. "He lied!"

Angela pulled her hand away from the sugar bowl, resisting the temptation, and looked at Joanna. "About what?"

"He said he knew her too."

Angela grinned. "You can't fault him for that. My Cory

would do the same. If a pretty woman pretended to know him he—"

"She wasn't that," Joanna said in a flat voice.

"What?"

"Pretty. She may be interesting, but certainly not attractive." Joanna shivered. "But there was something about her."

"Go on," Angela urged when Joanna suddenly grew quiet.

"She was wearing an emerald ring."

"That doesn't mean anything."

"I think she might be..."

"She couldn't be."

"She was wearing his birthstone and we know what that could mean."

Angela waved her hand. "A coincidence. There are a number of women who could be wearing his birthstone right now."

"I wouldn't have made much of it too, if he hadn't acted so strangely."

"The likelihood of a woman like that really existing is rare."

"But not impossible."

"No."

"I'm sure it's nothing," Angela said, taking another sip of her tea and trying not to grimace. It amazed her how much Joanna ignored her hints about how nice a change a glass of wine would be. "Don't fret. He'll go to sleep and forget all about it and you should too."

"But what if he starts to ask questions?"

"He doesn't know what questions to ask." She laughed. "We hardly know what to ask. Relax, nothing has changed and nothing will change."

"That's where you're wrong," a deep voice said from the doorway.

CHAPTER 13

The two women turned to him startled; Angela spilling tea onto her saucer, before setting it down.

James walked over to his aunt and kissed her sunken cheek before he pushed the plate of biscuits closer to her, hoping she'd take a few. Although fashionably dressed in a brown leather skirt and red silk blouse, she always had a gaunt, hungry look about her. "I didn't hear you come in," he said. He took a seat. "I was passing by and I couldn't help overhearing your discussion and since it's about me..." He shrugged. "I'm curious."

"Your mother was telling me what happened today."

"Oh, she told you about my decision to visit the office this week?"

Joanna looked at him alarmed. "You didn't tell me that."

"I'm telling you now. I also let grandmother know."

"Without consulting me?"

"She's very happy," he continued, ignoring her outraged tone. "She likes me showing interest in the business."

"You should have talked to me first."

"I didn't think I needed to."

"I like to know everything that goes on—"

James held up his hand. "Now you know."

His aunt sniffed. "There's no reason for you to visit the Design Studio. Everyone knows Cory's meant to take it over one day."

"That's not a given," James said in a careless tone.

Angela bristled. It was no secret that James was the Winfield golden boy: Brilliant and well liked by his uncles and adored by his grandmother, the powerful Winfield matriarch. Even though he was still young he had a determination and maturity that her son, Cory, lacked. If James set out to do so, he could take over everything and leave Cory and his two younger siblings dependent on him just as they were all dependent on Martha Winfield's good graces.

Angela knew it was only luck that kept her family safe. If the Winfields hadn't worried about James's health they would have put him in a position of power years ago. Fortunately, due to major health scares that began in his youth, Joanna kept a close eye on James, desperate not to lose him. "You have no real interest in the company."

James took a biscuit. "I have an interest in everything." He lifted the plate towards her, invitingly. "Take one."

Angela hesitated then found herself taking one in spite of herself. Then two then three.

"You're making your mother nervous. Is this your little way of rebelling?"

He flashed a grin. It wasn't quite cold, but it wasn't warm either. "I didn't realize I had to rebel to be a part of my family's business."

Angela lifted her tea. She didn't know where he'd gotten his voice from—like a man who'd lived for centuries and was wiser than all of them—but it always made her feel uneasy. Especially when she tried to outwit him. It was something she'd never managed to do and with one offhanded comment he'd effectively put her in her place. He may not have Cory's health, but he had a stronger will. But he was a considerate nephew and she knew it was unfair to distrust him.

"This summer was to be a holiday," Joanna said. "Eight weeks of rest before your next operation."

James leaned back in his chair. "I've cancelled it."

"What?"

"I don't want to discuss that right now—"

"You will. You can't think that because you're feeling better you can just neglect what the doctors have told you."

"I realized that I don't need it. I'm ready to live now. Most of my life has been tests, doctor visits, needles and surgeries." He sent her a look. "I'm not going back to that." He stood. "Now you can return to talking about me, but please keep your voices down." He left.

Joanna looked at Angela. "Did you see that? Did you see how he spoke to me?"

"It's a phase," Angela said, not too concerned about her nephew's behavior. The biscuits had been delicious and seemed to have put her in a better mood than before. "He's been good all his life, it's to be expected."

Joanna shook her head. "It's just not like him to keep secrets from me."

"I'm sure he keeps lots of secrets." She smiled at her sister's surprised expression. "He is a man after all."

"He's not an ordinary one."

"Any woman will find that out soon enough."

CHAPTER 14

A gerbil.

She hadn't given up a carefree summer to settle in a cheap London flat to become a gerbil, but that's exactly how she felt. *Serves you right*, she could imagine her second cousin Ginny saying. She was still miffed that Michelle had chosen not to stay with her family. She worked at a local greengrocer and her husband was a lorry driver. Michelle liked them both because they were warm, friendly people, but their flat was damp and overcrowded with relatives plus their three kids. They didn't have the space for her really, but were too proud to admit it. On the other hand, her mother's cousin had also offered her a place to stay, but more out of duty than true interest. He was a refined man who sniffed with the condescending air of a person who found anyone in his vicinity lacking proper hygiene.

Her present accommodations suited her. She had a flat mate who was never there and it wasn't too far from the office. Michelle made a paper clip chain at her desk while a light pattering of rain hit the office window. Unfortunately, her internship at the Winfield Design Studio was a cliché in the worse way

—data entry, running errands, paper work and little else. Although she hadn't expected much excitement being assigned to the Human Resources Division, she'd been able to get one of the other fifteen other employees (all women) to let her research local clients and candidates, analyze CV's and had been able to finagle one phone interview.

She'd quickly learned to evaluate candidates' skills and backgrounds even coming up with different questions to highlight possible skill sets missed through traditional evaluation. She had twice mentioned ideas (which might have saved them time and money) to her supervisor (the only man); seven times pointed out possible problems (which definitely would have saved them money), but her suggestions were ignored or summarily kept as the supervisor's keen idea to announce to the company president. But that didn't bother her because she didn't need the credit she knew she was bright, she just wanted more to do. More responsibility. She could get seven hours worth of work done in three and found herself bored the rest of the day. She hated boredom.

At least she knew that she still liked business. She liked the many different levels of it. She liked helping people with creative vision reach the market place, so she would continue pursuing her degree in business management with delight and eagerness. She had helped her father make extra money with his knowledge of stones, getting people to pay him for speeches and private sessions. She had an analytical mind and saw processes and opportunities others might miss. She didn't need the limelight, helping others gave her the greatest thrill.

But she was still bored. She had six more weeks before her summer internship ended and it seemed like eternity. Others would see her as lucky. An internship abroad would give her a world view, although, granted, she'd cheated a bit since she had family here. However, she had been forced out of her comfort zone by having to learn the tube system when she'd been used to the suburbs and driving everywhere, and seeing how the West Indian-British owned Winfield Design Studios handled business was an education in and of itself. The Winfields had been in business since the 1960s with offices and business interests here, in the US and other parts of the globe.

Perhaps she should have stayed stateside, but the weekend excursions proved worth the weekday boredom. She took her meager earnings and found as many low cost ventures she could find, which is how she managed the castle tour and had also visited Buckingham Palace and Regent Park. Next weekend she hoped to visit another landmark She didn't want to attend another castle or she'd think about James. The man she thought she'd made a connection with, but who had given her a bogus number. It had all seemed too good to be true anyway.

Michelle lifted her head when her supervisor left his office. Everyone else did the same. Cory Winfield was as good looking as he was lazy. And he was *very* good looking with hazel nut skin and short dark hair and a trim beard. He never remembered her name, or what she was there for or what *he* was there for at most times. But that didn't bother him or anyone else because he was the son of the president so most people didn't expect much from him and he expected even less from himself. However, he'd taken a particular shine to her because of her ideas and she'd managed to grab his attention by accident. Although she was told never to talk to him unless he talked to her first, when she'd spotted him in the hall with an important new client—Cory looking at him with a blank expression—she'd quietly fed him the client's name effectively gaining his appreciation.

"You make me look good," he'd told her one day when he'd caught her near the copy machine. He checked his perfect reflection in the side window. "I like that. The others don't do that."

He turned to her and winked. "I'll have a position waiting for you when you've finished university."

Michelle couldn't imagine wanting any position he could offer her. He was only one year older so it was difficult to take him seriously.

"Thank you."

"Don't thank me, say you'll accept."

She only smiled. He nodded. "Okay, I won't push you, but give it a thought, yeah?"

She nodded then left.

"Whadide satoou?" her colleague Tansy Finley said when Michelle returned to her desk. Tansy had been one of her early champions, doing her best to make Michelle feel at home. She had pale skin, hair as black as an oil slick and deep red lipstick.

"I'm sorry?" Michelle said feeling guilty. It was her frequent response to Tansy because she didn't always catch the words in Tansy's Scottish brogue.

Fortunately, she was patient. "I said, what did he say to you?" When Michelle told her what Cory had said, she'd sighed. "You are so lucky."

Unfortunately, she didn't feel lucky. She felt restless. What she was doing was all so easy. Even seeing Cory leave with his latest leading lady—she'd already seen him with two others in three weeks—wasn't interesting, although he was always the talk of the office. Who was he seeing now? Where was he going? Everything came easy to him and that was fine. But she wanted a challenge.

Michelle sat at her desk, having completed another coffee run for the day—the kitchen had a coffeemaker but most people avoided it as they would a sewage pit—wondering what activity she could make up as she watched Cory talk to one of her colleagues—a no nonsense, middle aged woman with thin framed glasses who looked like she could bench-press a Mini Cooper. Cory tended to avoid this woman, so the fact that he hadn't, caught Michelle's attention. It was while watching them that Michelle sensed a certain change in the air. The carefree nature disappeared; the atmosphere became tense. She looked at Tansy as she rushed past towards the conference room. "What's going on?"

"His cousin is here."

Michelle didn't know why that was important. No one had mentioned Cory's cousin before, but as she saw people clearing their desks—gathering up sweet wrappers, quickly replacing stuffed toys with framed photos of smiling babies, dressed up pets or holiday pictures, and watering neglected plants, Michelle looked at her own desk. There was not much to clean since her desk was devoid of any personal objects making it clear to everyone that her position was temporary. She only used the top surface anyway because the previous owner had, for some unknown reason, stuffed one of the drawers with Tampax boxes and the other with sugar biscuits and hand wipes. Michelle was not curious to know why.

Instead of tidying, she put her paper clip chain away and sat straighter. She glanced at Cory who looked oddly put out—like a grounded child. She'd never seen him frown before, except when a specific watch order had been delayed by a day. He'd sulked for hours. He caught her eye and walked over to her desk, his hands shoved in the pockets of his light khaki trousers.

"I need you to work your magic," he said in the low voice as if they were coconspirators.

Michelle shook her head, not understanding him. "Magic?"

"Make me look the best and you'll never have to look for employment again. That other girl is setting up the conference room for you."

"For me?"

He nodded. "You're going to tell them about that new software I implemented and the two new hires." He turned before she could respond. It annoyed her that he assumed that she worried about employment or that she even thought of him as an option. But she gathered her things and headed to the conference room where Tansy had set everything up. She shivered. The room was freezing, as always. It was rumored it had been set at that temperature to keep people awake. Michelle glanced at the filled water glasses surprised they hadn't turned to ice. She lined up one of the chairs around the table to keep her hands from going numb.

"I don't understand why this is such a big deal," Michelle said to Tansy. "Isn't he the son of the owner?"

"Yes," Tansy said, making sure the audio/visual was working, "but it's complicated. Don't be nervous."

How could she be nervous when she didn't know what was going on? At least she wasn't bored. She looked forward to the unexpected presentation. She'd wanted responsibility and now it was hers.

They waited by the wall, intermittently rubbing their hands to keep warm, when the main entrance to the conference room opened. An attractive older woman entered, wearing a gorgeous purple suit and black heels. A woman who looked familiar.

"I know her," Michelle said, watching the woman take a seat of prominence at the head of the table.

"Really?" Tansy said amazed. "That's Ms. Winfield. Oh...I didn't think he'd really come."

Although the older woman intrigued her, it was the man who followed that stopped Michelle's heart and let her know that this day would be like no other. It was James, the man from the castle, but there was no weakness about him. He had a masterful strength; he made Cory look like a child. She didn't mean to stare, but the transformation was remarkable. He scanned the crowd with a cursory acknowledgement, brushing past her before he stopped and looked again. A double take.

Just like before.

Except more powerful. She swallowed. His eyes met and held hers for seconds that felt like years then looked away. The moment was brief. No one else had noticed. But the room no longer felt cold. He remembered her. Would he say anything? Did it matter? She had to focus on the presentation. *Make me look good*, she could silently hear Cory beseech her. Cory walked over to her and whispered, "I know the room is bloody freezing, but try not to look like that."

"Like what?"

"You're frozen."

She took a deep breath. "Sorry."

"You don't have to be afraid. Focus on my aunt and ignore my cousin. He always looks fierce but he won't bite." He walked to the center of the room, flashed a charming grin and said, "Mindy is going to let you know what we've been doing."

Mindy? Really? He couldn't even try to get her name right?

"Why?" Ms. Winfield said.

Cory faltered, searching for an answer. "Why?"

"Yes, why is..." She made a motion with her hand and addressed Michelle without looking at her. "What's your name again?"

Michelle sent a glance at Tansy then Cory wondering how to respond. She couldn't let them know he'd made a mistake. "It's Michelle, but people call me Mindy for short," she said in a low voice.

Ms. Winfield nodded, her gaze fixed on her nephew. "Why is she presenting to us?"

"Because..." Cory tugged on his collar, sending the woman a desperate look.

"It's his generosity," Michelle said. "I need a certain amount of hours to do presentations."

Ms. Winfield finally shifted her gaze to her then paused, studying her for a long moment. "Have we met before?"

"Perhaps you passed her in the hall," Cory said. "She's been here several weeks." He nodded towards Michelle as a signal to begin.

Somehow, despite her racing thoughts, Ms. Winfield's eyes and James's powerful presence, Michelle managed to make it through the presentation as well as the pointed questions Ms. Winfield asked her. James remained silent. When the presentation was through, Ms. Winfield exited but James stood by the door, holding it open for everyone, making everyone shrink a little as they passed him.

Michelle refused to do so. She lifted her chin and headed out the door with her back ramrod straight. As she walked passed him he whispered low enough for only her to hear, "Do you believe in fate now?"

CHAPTER 15

Michelle fell into the chair behind her desk, her skin tingling. Coming from the freezing cold conference room the rest of the office felt like a sauna.

Cory came over to her, grinning. "Brilliant. I knew you would be."

"I'm not sure I impressed them."

"Would I be standing here grinning like this if you hadn't? Don't worry and relax. It's not like you to look scared. Although, admittedly, my relatives can be fierce."

She nodded again, unable to speak. She wasn't afraid. How could anyone be afraid of James? He was awe-inspiring—like a vast moonless night, sunlight on the surface of an ocean. And he was vulnerable. She'd never forget the feeling of weakness she'd sensed when she'd touched his arm, his heavy breathing when he'd run after her, his inability to speak at first. But even though his body may betray him, his eyes were too knowing, too wise.

She never thought she'd see him again and she couldn't believe how happy she felt. It was stupid. Their lives were so different. When he'd asked for her number it had been a moment of weakness. And a trick. The number he had given her hadn't been real. Now he'd know she was a nobody, a little intern in one of his family's companies. It was the extreme temperature change that kept her heart racing. Perhaps she needed something to eat. She absently opened her desk drawer to grab a biscuit then realized she'd opened the tampon drawer instead. She shrugged. If she was going to take a biscuit, she could take a box home as well. She opened the drawer and lifted up a small carton to slip it into her bag. It would save her money and no one would notice.

"Ms. Clifton?"

Her head shot up. She dropped the box back in the drawer and shut it, her face burning. *Did he see it? Please don't let him have seen it.* "Yes, Mr. Winfield?" she said, hoping her voice sounded appropriately professional. Was he going to compliment her presentation? Ask her questions about the software?

"Are you free tonight?"

Michelle stared up at him certain she'd misheard him due to the sound of her heart pounding in her chest. "I'm sorry?"

"Are you free tonight?"

"To work after hours?"

He sighed. "Why are you making this difficult? I'm asking you out."

Michelle surged to her feet, her heart racing. She looked around, knowing that the others were pretending not to listen, before she said in a low, frantic voice, "What are you doing?"

"I believe I just told you."

"Right now? Here?"

"If you'd given me your number, I would have been more discreet. Is that a 'yes' or 'no'?"

She would accept for the sake of appearances. The more she

prolonged the conversation the worse the situation would be. "Of course Mr. Winfield."

"James. You can call me James." He gave her the time then said, "I'll pick you up."

"But you don't know where I live."

He only smiled and she realized it wouldn't be hard for him to find out. "Until then," he said before he left.

Tansy turned in her chair and stared at Michelle wide eyed.

"It's probably for business," Michelle said before she could say anything, organizing papers on her desk that didn't need organizing. Her hands shook, her mouth felt dry. She didn't know what she was doing. Was this real? Had he really asked her out? Had she really said yes? Why had he been so public about it?

"He told you to call him James."

"Yes, well..."

"I'd be careful," the Mini Cooper woman said with a shake of her head. "Interns get their hearts broken all the time."

"By the likes of Cory," Tansy said. "Never him. It's never happened before."

"There's a first for everything."

"WHAT WERE YOU DOING?" Joanna demanded when James joined her in the backseat of their black Mercedes. Graham sat at the wheel and started the car. As he pulled from under the embankment the rain pounded the windscreen.

"I was talking to someone."

"And who was that?"

"Someone interesting."

"Well that couldn't be your cousin then. I've seen bobble head dolls with more substance."

"Cory has his charms, but you're right. It wasn't him."

Joanna frowned at him. "You look satisfied about something."

"I am." He was more than satisfied. He was on top of the world. He had found her again. Michelle. He hadn't been able to take his eyes off her as she did her presentation and hardly heard a word she said. But he knew it would be intelligent and he liked her poise. When their eyes first met in the conference room he felt her recognition. She knew who he was and he wouldn't allow her to pretend that she didn't. This time she wouldn't escape him so easily. He hadn't meant to walk up to her desk at first, but something had pulled him there and when her startled brown eyes met his he was enchanted once again. Eager to be by her side. It had been a calculated risk to make his intentions known so publicly, but he felt as if something else had taken over him and possessed him to do it. To stake his claim.

"James!"

He turned to his mother with a start. "Sorry?"

"I was talking to you."

"I wasn't listening."

"Congratulations on stating the obvious."

He sighed. "I'm sorry."

"You know you frighten me when your mind wanders like that. The doctor says—"

"I'm fine, I was just thinking about something."

"Or someone."

His mother didn't need to know anything about his dinner date. "It was nice to be back."

"You don't even work there."

No, he had a virtual office and usually worked wherever he was at the time. And that varied. He scheduled his life around doctor visits and appointments. He envied his cousin's set routine. In time he would have an office of his own. "It's nice to be back all the same."

"What has gotten into you?"

It was maddening. It was crazy. It was wonderful. But he couldn't deny it—

He was in danger of falling in love.

CHAPTER 16

She felt like a princess. Michelle sat in the plush pink booths among the candlelit dining room of the exclusive Mayfair restaurant, finishing her chocolate ganache cake and ginger ice cream feeling as if she were in a fairytale with her own handsome prince. A prince who gazed at her as if she were dripping in diamonds, as beautiful as an exotic flower, and was a treasure he wanted to keep. The conversation had flowed, as if they'd known each other for years. She learned he was an only child, home-schooled, born in England but raised both here and abroad, settling the past ten years in the States. He'd come to England to recuperate after a surgery he wouldn't describe or elaborate on and she didn't ask questions because she didn't want to pry.

It didn't take Michelle long to learned that James preferred to listen rather than talk, especially about himself, and she felt comfortable sharing about her immigrant parents, the place where she'd lived all her life, her two sisters and what she was studying at university.

"How is it working at Winfield Design Studios?" he asked her.

She hesitated. She didn't want to tell him the truth. Cory was family after all. "It's a wonderful learning experience."

James grinned. "A true diplomat. I was really impressed by your presentation."

"Yes, well Cory let me take the lead."

James laughed. "You don't need to pretend with me. We all know that the only ideas in my cousin's head are the ones someone else put there and I say that with affection."

"Hmm."

"But I won't force you to say anything bad about him."

"What do you do?" Michelle asked eager to change the subject.

"Not much."

"You can't be as lazy as your cousin," she said then covered her mouth ashamed, realizing her mistake. "Wait, I didn't mean that."

"Yes, you did. And don't underestimate Cory's role. He gives the right image and perception, which serves the company. I am more of an idea person, strategizing new ventures behind the scenes or advising on where we need to cut our losses. I basically spot problems and seize opportunities. I still have a lot to learn but the family trusts me. By the way, I forgive you."

"Forgive me?"

He nodded. "For not taking my card." He shook his head. "You don't have to explain. I don't care. I'm glad you're here now. Although I'm a little disappointed that my pedigree is what convinced you."

Michelle stiffened insulted. She didn't want him to think she was a status seeker. "And I forgive you."

"For what?"

"For giving me a bogus number."

"Bogus?"

"Fake."

"I know what bogus means."

"I..." She paused, embarrassed to admit the truth. "I came back to find you, but you were gone. Then I saw your card on the ground and..." She looked down at her ice cream. "I did call you." When James didn't respond she glanced up at him. He stared at her, motionless in a way that made her uncomfortable. She lowered her head and hardened her tone. "You think I'm lying."

"No."

The single dark note in his voice made her look up again. "Good because I'm not."

"When did you call me?"

"Soon after," she said trying to appear nonchalant. "Perhaps a day or two." *That night.* She'd called him that night but she didn't want to sound overeager.

"I see."

"Yes, and a man answered and told me I had the wrong number. I tried again thinking I'd dialed wrong but the same man gave me the same message." She looked at him. "I felt such a fool. I thought maybe...I was angry at you for toying with me and..." She let her words trail off when she realized her wasn't listening. He didn't look distracted but it was clear he was thinking of something else. He absently stroked the stem of his dessert fork in a methodical, repeated manner. "I guess it doesn't matter now," Michelle said, more to herself than to him.

"Would you like anything else?" he suddenly asked, sounding like a polite host.

"N-no," she stammered not sure of his change in tone. "This is fine. Thank you."

James nodded in the same absent way before he stood and said, "Excuse me for a minute," and then left the table.

INCENSED. He was incensed. James walked outside into the bustling London evening and called Graham on his cell phone. "I have a few questions to ask you," he said in a calm voice once the line was picked up, "and I only want one reply. Yes or No. Understood?"

"What's this about?"

"Yes or No. Do you understand?"

"I think you—"

"If I have to repeat myself, start looking for employment elsewhere."

"Yes, sir."

James swore. "Cut that out. You know I hate when you call me that. Is my mother around?"

"No."

"Good." James took a deep breath. "Did I recently get a phone call from a certain young woman?"

"Your mother—"

James closed his eyes and said through tight teeth. "Yes or No?"

Graham sighed. "Yes, but—"

"Has following instructions become difficult with age?"

"No, sir."

"Are you trying to annoy me on purpose?"

"No, si— sorry."

"Divided loyalties are difficult. I understand that. The choice is yours. Do you still work for me?" James had changed the dynamics of their relationship, without his mother's knowledge, when he'd turned fifteen and no longer felt he needed a caretaker but an ally instead. He secretly paid Graham, as a reminder, from the proceeds of a lucrative property he'd inherited from his grandfather.

"Yes, but can I elaborate?" When James met his question with silence, Graham felt it was safe to proceed. "I thought you were being hasty and your mother was worried enough after you'd cancelled the latest surgery. I wasn't sure—" He stopped when he heard James clicking his tongue. "What?"

"You're confusing me with an idiot. I know exactly why you did it. So I'll offer you only one warning. Do something like this again, interfere with my personal life in the smallest way, and our arrangement is over. Am I clear?"

"Yes."

"I forgive you. Now make sure this is the best holiday I've ever had."

"How?"

"Stay out of my way."

"Is everything okay?" Michelle asked when James returned to the table.

"It is now. I apologize about the wrong number. My assistant confused you for someone else. A woman who has harassed me in the past. It won't happen again."

"Does that happen often?"

"What?"

"You being harassed by women?" For a moment he looked flustered, and the expression surprised Michelle enough to make her laugh. "Never mind. Don't answer that. I'm teasing."

He discreetly motioned to a waiter. "How long are you in London?"

"Six more weeks."

"Mind if I reserve every one of them?"

"Every one? You might get tired of me."

"I won't. I'd like to see you again as much as possible."

Michelle folded her arms. "I can't say yes because I'm not sure I want to spend that much time with you."

James lowered his voice, a seductive smile dancing on his lips. "I'll have to be more persuasive then."

"Yes."

"It will be a targeted campaign."

"Okay."

He leaned towards her, making a promise. "And I will win."

She unfolded her arms and leaned towards him. "We'll see."

"Free tomorrow?"

She laughed pleased he wanted to see her again so soon. "Yes," she said and suddenly six weeks didn't feel very long at all.

CHAPTER 17

James walked past the living room where his mother sat flipping through the pictures of a glossy magazine.

"Where did you disappear to?" she asked him, without looking up, as he headed for his room. When he didn't reply she raised her voice. "I am talking to you."

He paused then stared at her lowered head. "Don't interfere with this."

"With what?"

"Just don't."

She turned a page making no effort to look up at him, her tone sounding disinterested. "I have to know what you're talking about before I can agree."

"I'm going to be busy the next several weeks."

"You can't push yourself too much. You know how you can be. You get excited. Over work yourself and then—"

"I won't."

She tossed the magazine aside and looked at him with frustration. "You always say that."

"I'll be fine."

"You push and push and then collapse." She tapped her chest. "And *I'm* the one who has to pick up the pieces. To nurse you back to health."

"It's different this time. I won't...have an issue. Not with her."

His mother paused, pursing her lips. Her tone and gaze sharpening. "Who?"

James silently swore, he'd said too much. "Just someone." He took a step back. "Good night."

"Don't you dare walk away from me."

James kept walking.

She rushed after him and grabbed him by the shoulders, her nails seeming to sink through his jacket like claws. "Who is she?" Joanna spun him around with a vicious urgency. "I will not let anyone hurt you. I will not risk you—"

He grasped her arms, pulling her away from him. Her grip hurt, but he knew she didn't mean it. She was frightened. "Mum—"

Her eyes shone with unshed tears. "You have to be extra careful. You're still so young. You can't be too carefree. Don't think only of yourself, but of me and how much this family depends on you staying well. You can't risk a relationship. Not only because of—"

"I know what I'm doing." He held her gaze and lightly kissed her balled fists. "Don't interfere." He turned and left.

Joanna returned to her seat, her tears quickly drying up. James was becoming wise to her. Tears had worked so easily in the past. He would gather her close and soothe her, promising her whatever she wanted. *Don't interfere.* She curled her lip. That wasn't going to happen. She picked up her cell phone and sent a message to Graham instructing him to meet her. Seconds later he stood in front of her ready for orders. He still stood like an officer and would look sexy in uniform. But even though he could appear 'tried and true', when he had been a cop she knew he hadn't been an honorable one. He was as bent as they come, but smart. She liked smart. "James was out with a woman. Find out who she is."

"I suspect we already know."

"Who?"

"The young woman from the castle."

Joanna gripped the arm of her chair. "That's impossible. I thought you told me you intercepted her phone call."

"I did. They met another way."

"How is that even possible..." She paused as she remembered the presentation from this afternoon. "I thought she looked familiar. How frustrating. I should have paid more attention."

"He's a man now."

Why did everyone feel the need to keep reminding her of that? She knew that truth better than anyone. Had she not felt the strength of his arms around her when she hugged him? Heard the depth of his voice? Seen the maturity in his gaze? When he was a teenager she'd seen how the gaze of others had changed ordinary attention to interest. But no matter how he changed on the outside, James would always be her little boy. Someone who would always need her. Because he was different. She had to guide and protect him no matter what.

"I'm sure that if we leave them alone, this will disappear on its own," Graham said. "He knows what he has to do and his family matters to him. Let the leash go a little."

Graham was right. If she tried too hard she'd push James away right into this young woman's arms. But if he got too cocky, she'd remind him what was at stake. "Okay, we'll give them a little leeway. For now."

CHAPTER 18

J ames Winfield// 23:04
    I found her.
        Martha Winfield// 23:04
Don't be hasty. Can you be certain?
James Winfield// 23:04
Yes. Still in New York?
Martha Winfield// 23:04
I am.
James Winfield// 23:04
When will you be in London?
Martha Winfield// 23:04
I have no need to be in London.
James Winfield// 23:05
I think you'll want to meet her.
Martha Winfield// 23:05
Why?
James Winfield// 23:05
Because I plan to make her my wife.
Martha Winfield// 23:07

I'll make arrangements to be at the cottage. Don't do anything until I get there.

James Winfield// 23:07

You have until the middle of August. Love you.

Martha Winfield// 23:07

Spoiled boy. XX

CHAPTER 19

He'd convinced her.

After only one more date with James, a drive along a country road followed by a picnic, he'd convinced her that she wanted to spend all her time with him.

After three weeks, Michelle couldn't imagine a life where he wasn't in it. She was so happy it frightened her. Could this much joy be real? She had spent as much time as she could with James after work and they devoted as much time as they could together from Friday night until Sunday. He took her to see the White Cliffs of Dover, the British Museum, Stonehenge and they travelled along the Thames. The dark broody air that had once swirled around him—the boredom and disinterest—seemed to have disappeared, replaced by a man who seemed to take pleasure in the tiniest thing—from buying her a bouquet from a street vendor to sharing a sundae on a lazy summer afternoon.

And yet, at times, Michelle sensed something was wrong with him; that her pace was sometimes too fast for him. Once she saw beads of sweat on his forehead after climbing a simple hill, but when she tried to talk about it, he changed the subject. He wouldn't let her mention his surgery or need for rest and recovery. He would only smile and say "You're the best remedy for anything that ails me," and talk about something else.

So Michelle decided to be very careful about where he took her. She didn't want him overexerting himself. She knew other women might be put out by his weakness, but she didn't care. He made her happy and accepted her as she was and that was all that mattered.

"I'd love to visit a fruit market," Michelle called to him from her bedroom as she put in her earrings. She wore jeans, a green top and multicolored scarf. The earrings—costume jewelry, a little gaudy—she'd bought to match her Stanford Norman designer scarf and make him smile. He'd come by her flat to take her to an outdoor concert. "The weather is perfect, don't you think?" When he didn't reply, she walked into the living room and saw him on the couch, dressed in one of his stylish bespoke shirts, with his head back and his eyes closed. It was a position she was getting used to.

There were moments he looked exhausted. But now she wondered. Was he seriously ill? Had his last surgery been for a bigger problem? He looked a little peakish and it was only early morning. She lightly tapped him on the shoulder.

He opened his eyes and smiled at her, warming her heart and making her worry at the same time. "You look great." He started to stand but she stopped him with her hand. He frowned. "What's wrong? You're not ready yet?"

Michelle bit her lip and sat down beside him, covering his hand. "If you're not up to this we can cancel."

"No, I want to."

"Are you...okay?"

He hesitated. "If I weren't would that change anything?"

She took a deep breath. "How sick are you?"

James looked away for a moment. "I'm getting my strength back. It's just taking some time. I'm sorry."

"You don't have to apologize."

He lowered his head. "I've spent most of my life either in a wheelchair, a cast or leg braces." He looked at her. "When I was three-years-old I was playing in the driveway and someone, they say it was the gardener, didn't see me and backed over me. Shattered both my legs and I was in braces for years after. At six I tripped and fell down the stairs and broke my arm. Then when I was about nine I got a new bicycle. My mother had been worried but I was so excited. I rode down the street and...I honestly don't remember much." He shook his head. "I remember waking up in another hospital. Another couple of years of surgeries and hospital visits followed. I still sometimes have trouble with my knees since the accident, which needs to get fixed. Just this spring I managed to fracture my shoulder, but I should be able to lead a normal life. But because of my past injuries, I'm not in the best of shape and I tend to tire easily and that's hard for me to admit but I'm getting stronger...this trip was to be an escape. And it has been. You're the medicine I needed."

"Is that why you were home schooled?"

He nodded.

"And why you're still single? I mean a man like you—"

The corner of his mouth curved up in a smile. "It's only one of the reasons."

"What's the other one?" She squeezed his hand when he fell silent. "You can trust me."

He squeezed her hand in return and stood. "I know, but that's enough about me for one day. Let's—"

"You're not ready to tell me about your talent?"

He turned sharply to her, his voice cracked. "What?"

She patted the empty space beside her. "Are you still trying to manage it?"

He didn't sit. He stood frozen.

"James, it's okay."

"You sensed it?"

She nodded.

"Does it scare you?"

"Do I look scared?"

He took a deep breath. "Yes."

"It's because...I don't want to lose you. And I don't want you to push me away. I'm not afraid of you."

"Why not?'

"My father once told me that I would meet a powerful man torn between two worlds and that I would be his anchor. I didn't believe him."

Until now. He hadn't opened his mouth but the words came into her mind.

"Yes. Until now," she said so that he would know that she'd heard him.

He sat down amazed. *Really? That didn't scare you?*

She shook her head.

I can't read your thoughts or anything.

I know that.

His eyes widened. *You can do it too?*

Only with you. You're helping me. I've never done it before.

He rubbed his chin. *No, you're lying. No one has ever been able to talk to me like this.*

She only smiled.

I can see the past. Sometimes by touching things, sometimes it just comes to me.

Then why did you go to a place filled with history like a castle?

He laughed. *I'm in England. Everywhere is filled with history, plus...I was trying to test myself. I had an incident...*

What happened?

He lowered his gaze and said, "That's the problem. I don't remember."

"You have blackouts?"

He looked at her. "They started when I was nine. They don't happen often," he said quickly, "and never when I drive. You're safe with me."

"I know that. You don't have to keep telling me. But one thing puzzles me."

"What?"

"The first time we met, when we were in the garden, for a moment I felt as if I were transported into another time and there was this emotional bond that was so strong."

His compelling eyes held her still. "I felt it too. But that's the first time anyone has ever shared a memory connection with me."

"A memory connection?"

"That's the best way I can describe it. It's like seeing someone else's life but feeling it as my own. When I don't have the words, I tie myself with another emotional memory."

"You were trying to tell me how you felt?"

"Yes."

"When did you know you had this talent?"

He smiled.

"What?"

"I've never heard it called a talent before. More like a curse."

"You can do something amazing. It's a talent, you need to hone it. How old were you when you knew you were different?"

"I always saw things others didn't but my family thought I had a wild imagination. The telepathy I only do with a few people like my grandmother, but rarely."

"Do you ever make people think in ways they shouldn't?"

"No. Okay," he admitted when she didn't believe him. "When I was younger I was a little more reckless, but I'm not that way now. At times I'll make suggestions that they might make on their own if they weren't afraid to do it on their own."

"I should be afraid then."

He took her hand. "It's not mind control. I can't convince anyone do something completely against their nature. Sort of like you."

"Me?"

"I know what you can do."

"How did you know? You guessed from the first day, didn't you?"

He shrugged. "The same way you knew I was different. I felt it. When I'm with you the energy is...controlled. Calm."

"And when I'm with you I feel electrified, energetic."

He smiled. "A good match then?"

"The best."

CHAPTER 20

Cory hated when his father stopped by his flat unannounced. He especially hated when his Dad stopped by after Cory had spent the previous night pub crawling with two sisters from Barbados who liked his accent. He hated it even more when his father chose to storm into his bedroom, opened the blinds and told him he had five minutes to get dressed because he wanted to talk. He swore and rubbed his eyes.

His Dad had terrible timing. Cory left the warm comfort of his bed, crawled over one of his new lady friends, replacing the sheets when it slid off her bare bottom, and grabbed a robe. He quickly brushed his teeth before stumbling into the hallway. At least his hangover wasn't too bad. He didn't feel sick and his head only felt like it had gained half a stone.

He squinted at his father who sat on the edge of Cory's stylish mauve couch as if afraid it would eat him. At least his father didn't look angry, so he knew he wasn't in trouble. That was a relief. Cory yawned and scratched his cheek. His skin felt rough. He'd have to buy a new facial cream. "What's this about then?"

"Rumors."

Cory sat down. "Rumors?"

"Yes," his father said. "Rumors I should know about."

"Okay."

"Rumors that involve the family."

"Okay."

"Certain rumors like the one about your cousin."

Cory frowned. "Which cousin?"

"James."

"There's a rumor about James?"

"Yes, the one about him dating an intern in your bloody department!" His father picked up a couch cushion and threw it at him with such speed it hit Cory square in the face. "Something you neglected to tell me about."

Cory rubbed his nose. "No need for violence, Dad."

His father lifted another cushion.

Cory held out his hands in defense. "I'm sorry. I'm sorry."

His father replaced the cushion. "How sorry?"

Cory lifted a brow uncertain. "Very?"

His father frowned. "You don't even know why I'm upset."

"Because you hate rumors?"

His father lifted the cushion once more. Cory curled himself into a ball as his father whacked him on the back of the head. "Do you think I enjoy getting hysterical phone calls from my sister?" he said. "Do you think I like being ignorant of what's going on within my own company?!"

Cory continued to cover his head and said in a timid voice, "I'm sorry. Really." He cautiously lifted his head when he heard his father move away. "I didn't think much of it."

"Did you know about her before?"

"Before what?"

His father sighed with impatience. "Before she was an intern. It's possible that they've met before."

"I didn't know anything about it."

"What is she like?"

Cory laughed at his father's concern. "Aunty has nothing to worry about. She's not even pretty. James probably liked her presentation and wanted to know more."

"For nearly a month?"

Cory's brows shot up. "Has it been going on that long? Wow, that's longer than I thought."

His father folded his arms. "Apparently."

"Okay, okay," Cory said, realizing his error. Then his mind jumped to another possibility. What if James was trying to lure her away? She was smart and efficient. A great worker and if she could make Cory look good she could make James look even better. Or what if James was using her to spy on him and find out how he was doing? But if that had been the case his father would have come down on him sooner. Besides, she didn't seem that kind of girl. No, his aunt and father had the wrong end of the stick. James was trying to muscle into his territory. That was his only interest in the plain little intern. He'd have to remember to be extra nice to her. "I'll pay more attention. Do you want me to say something to her? Put a stop to it?"

"No, I want you to keep me informed." His father rubbed his chin, pensive. "You really don't think she's a threat?"

"Trust me, Dad. Mindy is not a problem."

CHAPTER 21

The jar of sweets was a surprise as well as the disarming grin Cory gave her when he placed it on her desk.

Michelle looked up at him confused. "What's this?"

"Just a little token to let you know how much you're appreciated," he said.

"I haven't really done anything."

He nodded. "So humble and modest. Don't forget that the offer I made is negotiable. I want you to be very happy here." He patted her on the shoulder then stopped and sent her a worried look. "That's not sexual harassment, is it? Dad's always going on about it, but a friendly pat doesn't count, right? It's not like I whacked you on the ass, which, of course, would be completely out of order and not something I would ever do. You can trust me. I am the kind of supervisor I hope you would feel comfortable coming to at any time. We do have a good relationship, don't we? I didn't make you feel uncomfortable, did I?"

"No, but all your questions are starting to."

"Right, back to work then." He left.

Tansy watched him go. "Well, he's walking straight, so he's not smashed."

"Drunk?" Michelle said, making sure she understood the meaning.

"Yes. What's with him?"

Michelle shook her head, lifting the jar of sweets. "I don't know."

"He's probably nervous about you dating his cousin," Mini Cooper said eying the jar of sweets.

Michelle handed it to her. "Take some and share it around."

To Michelle's surprise her face lit into a wide grin and she eagerly opened the jar. "Thanks." She pulled out a handful of sweets and stuffed them in her sweater pockets. "My advice still stands. Be careful not to get your heart broken." She turned and began offering the other workers the jar.

"How is it going with James?" Tansy asked, drawing out James's name in a dramatic fashion.

Michelle shrugged with nonchalance. "Oh, we're just friends. It's nothing special."

"I WANT you to meet my grandmother."

James's request surprised her. Michelle switched her phone to her other ear while she slipped out of her dress shoes. She was still recovering from Cory's strange behavior this morning, but James's words that night left her speechless. "Your grandmother?"

"Yes."

"I had no idea. She looks awfully young. When I first saw her I thought she was your mother." She certainly acted like it at the castle.

James paused. "Who are you talking about?"

"Ms. Winfield. The woman you were with at the Design Studio."

"Yes, she is my mother."

"Oh...but you want me to meet your grandmother?"

"That is correct."

He was skipping over his mother to his *grandmother?* Somehow that made her feel even more nervous. Wasn't there a protocol to follow? It was like skipping the main meal and going straight to dessert; entering a building and zipping to the penthouse suite. She knew a formal introduction to his mother would be an experience, but his grandmother would be ten times more. Michelle sunk into her couch feeling the weight of the responsibility and honor.

"You'll be fine. I'll pick you up Saturday." He told her the time but she barely heard it.

"What should I wear?"

"Just be yourself," he said then disconnected.

She immediately went out and bought a simple blue cocktail dress and matching shoes. James said she looked lovely, but he always said that so she didn't believe him. The true test would be his grandmother.

And Martha Winfield was everything Michelle had imagined her to be and more. She was as regal as a Benin statue and beautiful with a long slender neck, rich cocoa skin and a short afro as white as sugar. When Michelle saw Martha sitting in the living room of the Winfield's expansive country cottage—which to Michelle looked like a midsize castle—dressed in a golden white blouse and black skirt, flanked by two large woven baskets bursting with large peacock feathers, she had to resist the urge to curtsey or bow.

Martha held out her hand. "Let me see the ring."

James nodded when Michelle hesitated. "It's okay."

Martha laughed. "I'm not going to steal it. I only want to make sure."

Michelle looked at James uncertain. "Make sure of what?"

He folded his arms. "Just let her see the ring."

"No."

His hands fell to his hips. "What?"

"I said no."

What are you doing? He silently asked her.

I want to know what's going on.

Let her see the ring.

Why?

He cupped her chin. *Because I'm asking you nicely.*

Michelle narrowed her eyes. *And what happens when you stop being nice?*

"Okay, you two," Martha said. "Enough of that."

You'll find out soon enough. James said.

Michelle smiled. *I'm trembling.*

Martha clapped her hands. "I said that's enough." She held out her hand. "Let me see the ring. It's not a suggestion."

Michelle reluctantly pulled off her ring. She knew manners dictated respecting one's elders but she didn't like being bossed about. She watched Martha take out a loupe and inspect it. "Yes, it's genuine."

I could have told you that, Michelle wanted to say, but didn't. Her father may not be as rich as a king but he knew his trade.

"Where did you get it?"

"My father gave it to me."

"Why?"

"Because it was my birthday."

"There was another reason."

Michelle sighed not wanting to share her father's story with a stranger.

Go on and tell her, James said.

Michelle wanted to put her hands over her ears, but she knew that wouldn't help. *Will you cut that out?*

Please.

I have to think.

Stop being an arrogant American.

As opposed to a nosy Brit?

I prefer it to a haughty Jamaican.

Right now you're showing your true roots and being a condescending West African—

East actually.

I don't care.

Our children will.

What?

Never mind.

"I know it seems like a personal question," Martha said with a note of apology, seemingly oblivious to their exchange. "But it's important."

Michelle rubbed her hands together feeling foolish. When she'd been alone with James their connection seemed magical somehow, but under the scrutiny of an outsider it seemed as childish as one of her father's many tales. "My father thought the ring was a way for divine love to find me."

James looked at his grandmother, satisfied. "See?"

Martha nodded. "Yes, I do. Well done." She handed Michelle the ring. "Your father was right. You may find it strange that James would have you meet me, but he has to be very careful with his choice. Hold out your hands, palms up." She shook her head when Michelle opened her mouth. "No, need to argue. Bite your tongue and do as I asked."

Michelle bit her lip instead and held out her hands.

Martha looked at Michelle's palms. "You are a strong woman." She lifted her gaze to Michelle's face and slightly frowned. "It's a shame you aren't handsome, but you carry yourself well. Do you have siblings?"

"Yes, two sisters."

"Are they like you?"

"They have their own gifts."

"Is one a stone reader?"

Michelle clasped her hands behind her back, surprised by the question. "Yes."

"Hmm. Are your sisters married?"

"Too young."

"That's not an answer."

"Not yet."

Martha nodded. "So you'd be the first. That's good. Tell me the myth of your people."

"The myth?"

"Yes."

Michelle resisted the urge to roll her eyes, remembering the many times her father had forced her and her sisters to recite the tales. Although she liked the stories she never truly believed them. But if a wealthy woman wanted to be entertained, who was she to argue? Michelle cleared her throat, lifted her chin and stood as if she were on stage entertaining thousands. Then with the slow, captivating cadence of a storyteller she said, "It is said that my people came fully formed from the insides of a petrified tree when the God of Whispers cried because no one could hear his voice. We burst forth with a radiant array of gifts and learned to honor him by using the natural treasures of the earth to speak. Giving jewelry and other ornaments are vastly important to us because it speaks for both the giver and receiver, showing many different things. Sometimes love, sometimes destruction. We believe that when you possess something it becomes part of you." Michelle lowered her head, half-expecting applause.

Instead Martha stood, grabbed one of the peacock feathers and whacked Michelle hard on both shoulders. "I approve."

James rushed forward and kissed his grandmother on both cheeks. "Thank you."

"Yes," Michelle said, removing a peacock feather from her dress. "It was a pleasure to meet you."

Martha put the peacock feather back in the basket and said with a smile. "It's not time to say goodbye yet. We've only just started."

JAMES SQUEEZED Michelle's hand as they walked along the garden path at the back of the cottage. "You were great. She likes you."

"Because of the peacock feathers?"

He sent her a solemn look. "They're important."

She sighed. "I know. And I'm glad I passed whatever odd test that was. I half expected to walk into a room with twenty mattresses."

"What?"

"Like *The Princess and the Pea.*"

He frowned.

Michelle looked at him stunned. "You've never heard of *The Princess and the Pea?*"

He shook his head. "I grew up on stories like *The Lazy Tortoise.*"

"Oh," Michelle said realizing she'd never heard that story. She shook her head. "Doesn't matter, it wasn't my favorite anyway."

James smiled up at the blue sky above, and listened to the sound of a goldfinch singing from a tree. "I feel like a weight has been lifted."

"Has your talent really caused you that much trouble with relationships?"

For a moment a sad expression crossed his face then he looked at her and smiled. "The past doesn't matter anymore."

"When will you tell your mother about me?"

His expression grew guarded. "My grandmother is the only family who needs to know about this right now."

"Because you don't think she'll like me?"

James glanced at his watch. "We'd better get back."

"You're avoiding my question."

He sent her a long look. And again, like before, the garden seemed to melt away and she was again standing in the palace, but this time he didn't kneel before her. He stood before her, proud, powerful, dark; his compelling presence suddenly making her senses spin and a potent feeling of excitement swept through her as the man that she saw swept her into his embrace. And she felt safe and loved. But then arms grabbed her and then him and forced them apart. And she opened her mouth to scream but no sound came. And the ring on her finger seemed to glow as the vision faded away replaced by the sight and scent of hollyhocks and foxgloves. She looked at James, her heart racing. He had answered her question. There were people who would tear them apart. Her question no longer mattered, what anyone else thought no longer mattered. He hadn't moved, but everything between them had shifted. He was asking her to trust him.

"Ready?" he said.

She nodded knowing he was preparing her for a bigger test. "Yes."

CHAPTER 22

Dark forces still swirled but there was a chance at happiness.

A slim chance.

Martha watched James and Michelle walk hand-in-hand in the garden but she knew they were no ordinary young lovers. In truth she doubted they were lovers at all, yet. Her grandson would be very careful about that. He would dazzle Michelle so much she wouldn't know what she was missing—until she did. But by then James would know what to do. Her grandson had been surrounded by darkness all his life, he deserved a chance to capture light—joy. Something that had been missing from his life for years. The Seer had a described woman like Michelle offering him a chance.

"You're being cruel. Why would you approve a match that could never be?"

Martha turned to her friend and companion, Hildie Buxton, who had a disposition like sour butter. She was a large woman with small feet, a wide nose and heavy eyebrows who had been by Martha's side for decades and knew all her secrets.

"It's possible. Shame she's not pretty."

"She's prettier than you are."

Martha smiled, liking her friend's honesty. It was true. Michelle had an inner beauty Martha certainly lacked and she had done plenty of acts she would later atone for. But power came with casualties. She had done what she had to survive. Those who didn't survive, died.

"She will have to find out."

"Not if it's not necessary."

"How long will you keep them both in the dark?"

"As long as it takes."

"He's getting stronger."

"I know."

"That puts him at risk."

"Then this young woman came into his life just in time."

CHAPTER 23

He didn't love her.

It was a painful thing to admit, but Michelle forced herself to face it. In four days she'd return home. This was their last weekend together, but despite the time together and visiting his grandmother, she knew this was not real. That she cared about him more than he did her. Because not once had he touched her as a man in love with a woman.

Michelle sat on the blanket while James lay next to her with his eyes closed. She looked out at the Cambridge campus where other couples lazed, rode bicycles and one group threw a Frisbee. She'd miss him. She loved him. She didn't want their time together to end. But it had to because it was all make-believe. *You better prepare yourself for heartbreak*, Mini Cooper had warned her. She hadn't listened and now she would pay. She jumped when she felt a warm hand against her cheek.

"No, don't do that," James said in a soft voice, wiping away a tear.

Michelle rubbed her eyes embarrassed. She wasn't one to be emotional. Crying was silly. She plastered on a smile and laughed. "I'm just so happy right now. It's all so perfect." His gaze stayed on her face. She lowered her head suddenly feeling shy. "Why do you do that?"

"What?"

"Stare at me that way?"

"What way?"

She managed to look at him. "Like you're entranced or amazed by something."

"Because I am."

She sniffed unimpressed. "Don't say it's because I'm beautiful because I know I'm not."

"No, you're something so much more." He sat up, his tone eager. "I don't want to lose you again."

"Long distant relationships are hard." She frowned when he started to smile. "What?"

"It doesn't have to be long distance."

"What do you mean? You're here and I'm—"

He shook his head. "I don't have a fixed address. Yet."

"Yet?"

He nodded. "For most of my life I've lived near the best hospital or specialist. We have different properties so I'm used to moving. I don't care where I land."

"What are you saying?"

"Meaning, where you are I'll go."

"But I live in this unexciting town in Maryland."

He nodded. "Okay, we'll settle there."

"You make it all sound so simple."

"It's not but it's worth it." He drew her close and held her tight. "I want this. I want this always."

She smiled, resting her head on his chest. "A moment captured forever."

"I'm serious."

She stared at a yellow car passing in the distance. "About what?"

"Marrying you."

She turned sharply to him.

"If you'll have me."

She stared at him not knowing what to say.

"Unless you want to live together first."

She opened her mouth then closed it.

"I'm getting stronger and—"

Michelle shook her head. "It's not that. I know you're strong." She gripped her hand into a fist. "It's just...are you sure?"

"Yes. I've been thinking about this for a long time. This feels right. No matter what trials we'll face, we can face them together."

"But you're gay."

He blinked. "I'm what?"

She turned away and laughed with cynicism. "Of course marrying you would work since you're not afraid of me and I'm not afraid of you. And arrangements like this have been made for centuries."

"Michelle—"

"And I completely understand that you'd want to move away and live—away from your family. Especially your mother. But I don't think you'll be happy hiding who you really are."

James shook his head. "Michelle—"

"It's okay," she said tears filling her voice. "I suspected it and I understand why you chose me. I should be grateful but I'm not. I love you and not just as a friend. I'm greedy and want to be with a man who truly loves me too."

"I'm not gay."

"I've been with you all these weeks and you've never kissed me."

He took her hand and smiled. "I've kissed you on the cheek."

Michelle shook her head. "That's not the same."

"On the hand too."

"You can do that with anyone."

"I'm being a gentleman."

"I don't want a gentleman." She sighed. "I want someone who truly loves me."

"I do."

"As a woman."

He closed his eyes and took a deep breath. "I do."

Michelle opened her mouth to respond when she felt herself back in the palace again with him and he spoke to her with words she didn't understand, but felt in her heart. She angrily pulled her hand away from him and the vision disappeared. "I don't like being manipulated."

"It's how I feel."

"Show me how you feel."

"I just did."

"No, right now. In this time." She touched his arm, lowering her voice to a seductive purr. "You know you want to. You want to be with me. You want to touch me and taste me."

James shook his head as if trying to clear her effect on him. "Stop it."

"You're strong. Strong enough for anything and you've been so patient. Waited so long. Now it's your chance."

He looked at her, his dark gaze burning. His voice a ragged gasp. "Not yet."

"Kiss me."

His gaze heated. *I won't be able to stop.*

Yes, you will.

And I'll want to make love to you.

I won't mind. I want you to.

He shook his head. *You don't know what you're asking. We have to wait otherwise you won't have a choice. You'll be bonded to me for life.*

Do you love me?

There will be no turning back. I mean it. The ceremony won't matter, the guests, nothing. You'll be mine. Completely. Always.

Michelle wrapped her arms around his neck. "Is that a promise?"

CHAPTER 24

He was going to lose her tonight. James felt an increasing feeling of doom crawl over his skin as he walked inside his private flat. He held the door open for Michelle to pass. He closed the door, hearing the soft click as the lock engaged. *Take her*, a sinister voice whispered. *Take her and don't look back. She said she wanted it. Said she wanted you. Make her prove it.*

He'd been with women before. Two he'd paid for and one... One who'd been a mistake. He'd gotten cocky and scared her. He had to be careful not to scare Michelle.

But you will. The voice said again. *Because she means too much to you. You won't be able to stop yourself.*

"Would you like something to drink?" he asked her. Michelle jumped and he couldn't blame her, his voice sounded extra harsh even too his own ears. He didn't know what came over him when he was in this space, but he didn't dare take her to his family's flat. He was too old to be slipping in undetected like a teenager. This place had been his small taste of freedom, though he rarely used it.

He turned to Michelle who seemed frozen in the foyer, her

gaze sweeping around the room. He'd had one of his mother's designers construct it in a modern style of silver and black. "Take a seat." She didn't move. Her eyes were wide, she was frightened. He could feel it. But he stood blocking the door, blocking her escape. He couldn't let her go. "What's wrong?"

Michelle's brows furrowed. "Are you sure you live here?"

"One of the many places," he said, taking her hand and leading her to the couch, feeling the hunger inside him growing. She smelled good. He knew she would taste even better.

Michelle sat down, but continued to survey the room with unease. "It doesn't feel like you."

James cupped her cheek and forced her to face him. "But it is me," he said in a velvet whisper. He felt her tremble and a rich, raw excitement gripped him.

She covered his hand with hers. "Are you sure?"

He paused, the hunger ebbing a little. She wasn't supposed to ask questions like that. Or look at him like that either. *She's trying to control you. Don't listen.* He bent to kiss her.

She turned her head and pressed her hand against his chest, stopping him. "No, James."

Anger shot through his veins. "You lied to me."

She lifted her hand to his face and met his eyes. "No," she said in a steady voice.

James sent her a hooded glance. "You've changed your mind."

Michelle shook her head and continued to hold his gaze. She spoke in a soft voice. "No. You did." He started to shake his head, but she stopped him and her voice remained calm and steady. "You've changed your mind because this isn't what you wanted. This isn't how you wanted it."

James closed his eyes wanting to fight her words, feeling the affect they had on his hunger. But another part of him knew she was giving him—them—a way out.

He opened his eyes and stared at her for a long moment before he said in a hoarse voice, "Go." When she didn't move, he added, "Quickly before I convince you to stay. I'll meet you at the car."

"James—"

His eyes flashed but he didn't raise his voice. "Now." *Before I can't stop myself,* he added sending her the urgent, silent message.

Michelle quickly grabbed her handbag and raced out the door.

James hung his head, feeling the pain of what he'd lost.

MICHELLE PACED OUTSIDE of James's flat, her heart pounding. She felt awful. Had she lost her courage? No, she wanted him still. But something felt wrong. Terrifying.

There had been no apprehension when she'd first arrived at his place. She'd been eager, but the moment she'd crossed past the door and entered his place something fearsome gripped her. She remembered clasping her hands together against the dark chill. The décor didn't suit him, although it was masculine, sophisticated and modern, there was a large ornate mirror against the far wall and a hutch crowded with crystal figurines that seemed out of place. Plus, there was something in the air that made her feel uneasy. Uncertain. Afraid.

And then she saw James's face. Something about his expression had changed. It seemed hungrier, more primal. What was going on?

James opened the door then stopped when he saw her. "I told you to wait in the car," he growled.

She didn't move. She searched his features relieved to see the animalistic, primal hunger was gone from his face. He looked like himself again. She grabbed his arm. "Promise me not to go back in there."

He pulled his arm away and headed down the hall. "Let me take you home. Unless you're afraid—"

"There's something bad in there."

He shrugged. "It's up to you."

"I want you to take me home. You can stay at my place."

He tapped the side of his head. "Do I look completely daft?" He motioned to the door. "Do you think I want to repeat what just happened? I may be wrong, but I'm pretty sure there aren't too many men out there who enjoy the sight of their girlfriend racing out of their arms in terror."

Michelle shook her head feeling miserable. "It's not you. I wasn't running from you. It's..." *That place,* she thought. But she didn't know how to express it. Her fears didn't make any sense. She'd never had such a strong reaction to a place before. That was Teresa's territory. Teresa was the sensitive one. Nothing usually shook or scared Michelle. But she'd sensed something in that place, something that seemed to take over him. Had her heart led her wrong? Had it all been a mistake? He'd twice wondered if he frightened her. Was there another side to him she hadn't seen? Had he kept it hidden by not being intimate with her? She had to know the truth. She grabbed the front of his shirt and kissed him. And the moment their lips touched, a delicious, warm sensation filled her body. She deepened the kiss and he groaned low in his throat arousing her more.

He drew back. "No."

She snaked an arm around his neck then softly stroked the back of his head. "But you want this." She pressed her body against his, feeling how much he wanted it. "You want it so bad."

"Don't do this to me," he said in a raw whisper. "Don't run—"

She flicked her tongue against his lips. "Do I look scared?"

His large hands drew her body closer. "Maybe I should be," he said before he covered her mouth with a passionate possession.

She moaned, her knees feeling weak, her hand sweeping his back wanting to feel his naked flesh beneath her fingers.

James moved his mouth to her neck, his voice warm when he spoke. "We can't do this here."

"I know. Stay at my place tonight."

He hesitated.

She toyed with the hair at the nape of his neck. "You want to."

James captured and held her gaze. *Careful Michelle, your trick won't work so easily the second time.*

I won't run.

You better hope not, he said, softly brushing his thumb over her lips.

I won't.

His gaze lit with satisfaction. *Good because this time, I won't let you.*

Michelle changed out of her clothes at a speed she never thought possible. She heard James bumping around in the tiny bathroom as she scrambled to undress. He'd asked to use the toilet then disappeared in there the moment they'd reached her flat. She didn't know what he was up to but at least he was there. Tonight was the night. He said he wasn't gay, and from his kiss to the feel of his arousal she believed him, which was good. So that meant he truly was attracted to her, loved her, and wanted to spend his life with her.

Success!

If only she had sexy lingerie to celebrate. Unfortunately, she hadn't prepared that far. She slipped on a blue camisole and matching pajama bottoms, jumped into bed, and slid under the covers. She took a deep breath. Everything would be okay now.

She closed her eyes when she heard the bathroom door open. *Play it cool. Play it cool.* He wanted this as much as she did; there was no need to be nervous. She felt the mattress shift as it accommodated his weight and she became aware of how narrow the bed was. Drats, it would be really embarrassing if she fell out. She also realized he was naked, feeling the power of his arousal through the fabric of her clothes. She felt his arm snake around her waist, then he said in a low whisper. "Are you chilly?"

"What? No."

"Do you think I'm a magician then?"

She turned to him. "I don't understand what you're saying."

"You're wearing pajamas."

"I know that."

"Are they...uh...a special kind?" His hand slid between her legs and stopped at her center.

Michelle gasped, shocked by the feel of his hand there. She shoved it away. "What are you doing?"

"I thought they'd be crotchless."

Michelle's voice cracked. "Why would they be crotchless?"

"How else do you expect me to be with you?"

She frowned. "You are with me."

"Inside you," he corrected.

"Oh..." Michelle said, drawing out the word as she came to an understanding.

James eyes gleamed with tender amusement. "First time?"

"No," she lied.

He nodded. "Yeah, it's not my first time either."

Her eyes widened. "Really?"

James started to smile and she realized he was trying to catch her in a lie. She shimmed off her pajama bottoms, her cheeks burning. "I *was* a little chilly."

"That's what I thought."

He shifted a little and the bed squeaked in protest. "This is going to be quite the balancing act."

"I'll just hold on to you."

There was laughter in his voice when he spoke, "Yes, you do that."

"Should we turn off the lights?" she wondered, looking around her shabby flat in dismay. It was clean and serviceable but far from elegant and definitely not romantic. She wouldn't think of where he'd been with woman before. Likely in king sized beds with fine sheets and the scent of roses not coconut lotion and barbecue crisps.

"It's up to you."

"Right," she said then realized she'd taken off her pajama bottoms and tossed them out of reach. So she'd be walking half-naked to the light switch giving him a complete view of her backside. She had a great figure, but she wasn't that comfortable yet. "I'm fine."

"Do you want me to stay where I am?"

"Sorry?"

He chuckled. "Where do you want me? Front, back, side?"

How would I know that? Why so many questions? I honestly don't know what I'm doing! But she didn't want to admit that. She was someone who took control. Who assessed a situation and knew the next move. She didn't want to appear weak. Vulnerable. Wasn't making love supposed to be easy?"

It's okay. I won't ask any more questions.

Michelle stared at James horrified. He'd heard what she'd said? She narrowed her eyes. *You said you couldn't read thoughts.*

He lifted his brows. *I can't. You told me.*

I didn't tell you anything!

You said it out loud.

I didn't. But she might have let her guard down and told him instead of just thinking it. She'd have to learn to be extra careful with him in the future.

Let's argue later. James threw one bare leg over her thigh, pressing the length of his body on top of hers before she felt the heat of his mouth. With his leg, he pried her legs apart, but he didn't enter her right away. There was a teasing, playful rhythm between them—him, like waves crawling up a sandbank and withdrawing again and her, the ocean, wet, dark and willing. Then he was inside her and she felt a rush. A fiery possession as their bodies connected in exquisite harmony. Then she felt as if a gush of wind had burst through the window and threatened to sweep them away, and she held on tight trying not to be overwhelmed by the sensations swirling around her. The room disappeared and all that was left was space and sky. And him. An all encompassing force.

I won't be able to stop. That's what he'd warned her. And now she knew what he meant. That this unleashed power swirling around them was him—his talent was taking them beyond space and time to pure energy. Potent energy that threatened to consume her, but she wasn't afraid because her body had been designed for it. With every fiery touch of his mouth, of his hand, of his chest, her body cooled it into submission. He was not too much for her. He was perfect. No ordinary man could incite such sweet pleasure.

To her, this was ecstasy—the feel of his large hand sweeping across her stomach, the sweet taste of his tongue inside her mouth, the hard, sleek caress of his body.

His body. James groaned deep in his throat as Michelle's cool fingers splayed across his back as she tightened around him, inviting him deep into the sacred space between her thighs. A healing space. With her he was a man once more not a...no he wouldn't think about that now. That was in the past. He had a future now. He had found her. He had found his equal: The one who could keep him from going over the edge and sinking into the darkness below.

He surrendered to his need for her and she surrendered to a need she never knew she had. A bond she knew she could never break. Their souls took hold of each other, intertwined—forever.

CHAPTER 26

J ames Winfield// 08:35
She said yes.
Martha Winfield// 08:35
Have you told her everything?
James Winfield// 08:35
I'll need your help.
Martha Winfield// 08:35
It's a risk.
James Winfield// 08:35
I know. Will you help?
James Winfield// 08:37
I'll live with the consequences.
James Winfield// 08:38
I'm going to marry her.
James Winfield// 08:42
Please help me.
James Winfield// 08:45
Please Gran. She's leaving tomorrow.
Martha Winfield// 08:55

Okay.

Martha shook her head and set down her phone with a sigh. She looked out the window of her bedroom alcove.

"What's the sigh for?" Hildie asked, picking up the breakfast tray. There was still a slice of toast and three slices of cut orange left. Martha knew they'd disappear before the tray reached the kitchen. Hildie hated to waste food.

"James wants to get married. He's asked for my help."

Hildie set the tray down with a clatter. "You let it go too far."

"I'm going to help him." She held up her hand before Hildie could argue. "He pleaded with me. He said 'please' twice."

And her grandson didn't ask for much. There had been so many—too many—times that he'd asked for her help—when he was four, six, ten, fifteen, twenty—and she'd been unable to do anything. "Please make the pain stop," he'd cried more than once, tears streaming down his face as he lay in a hospital bed. "Please make me better Gran." "Please make the doctors go away. I'll be good. Please. Please. Please."

And then there had been the times when she could have helped him but had refused. "Please let me ride with you. Please let me sail with you. Please let me live with you."

But that had been a foolish request. A child was meant to stay with his mother. No matter how smothering at times that person could be. But now he wanted freedom. He wanted to finally be his own man and he'd found the right woman. She would give him his wish and hoped they both didn't regret it.

MICHELLE FOUND herself somewhere over the Atlantic thinking about James. She remembered the tearful goodbye she'd had with Tansy, promising to keep in touch, and the big, awkward hug from Cory, who had repeated his offer of employment. But it was James who filled her thoughts. She remembered their parting at Heathrow.

"I'll join you in a day or two," he said, keeping his distance from her. "I have to take care of a few things here. Then we'll get married."

"But your family—"

"My grandmother knows and that's all that matters. The rest of my family won't understand so they can't know about us. Not until after."

"Are you sure—?"

"It's the only way we can be happy. Trust me. This is the best way we can be together."

He kissed her on the forehead then briefly—wonderfully—he smiled at her and the airport fell away and they stood yards apart on a dusty road on a Caribbean island and he was in uniform and she felt as if she were sending him away.

Don't worry. I'll come back. I love you.

I love you too.

And the solider, who was him but not him, embraced her erasing all her fears. But now, high above the clouds, she wondered about his urgency, his secrecy and whether they would ever be together again.

SHIT! The little weasel had slipped through his fingers and now Joanna would give him hell. Graham stared at James's bed that hadn't been slept in. He opened the closet and expected to see empty hangers, instead it looked the same as always. The same as James's private London flat when he'd visited. Graham hadn't suspected a thing. But he should have paid more attention.

James's behavior had become too routine. His time with the Clifton girl had appeared to be a banal diversion. Graham had followed them four times (without James knowing) until he realized there was nothing really interesting between them. Boring actually. They didn't even look like a couple. No pub-hopping, no club visits. He actually felt sorry for the plain girl. Seemed she was so desperate for attention that she'd take anything.

Even a weakling like James. A man who only kissed her on the cheek, maybe once on the forehead. Briefly, Graham wondered if James had ever been intimate with a woman before. But he knew he had since he'd provided him with an escort when James was nineteen. Every guy needed to get his experience somehow, right? And James was curious.

And this was how the kid repaid him? By lying. James had come back at the regular time, but clearly hadn't been staying there. For the past couple of weeks James had been feeding him false intel and he'd fallen for it. James hadn't trusted him as much as he'd thought. Smart kid.

Damn.

Graham turned when he heard the buzz of the front door. He half hoped it would be the police—what the hell were they called over here, bobbies or something?—telling them that James had been in an accident. It had happened before. But when he left James's room he didn't hear any unfamiliar voices or sense anything was wrong.

"Where is he?" Joanna demanded, when Graham returned to the dining room where he'd been eating breakfast before they noticed James was missing. He entered the room and saw that Martha and her companion Hildie had joined her; all three were sitting at the table, which was rare for a weekday morning. Martha preferred breakfast alone. "Is he sick?"

Graham pulled out his chair and sat. "He's not sick."

"But he's always on time for breakfast."

Graham sighed. He was going to need a big whiskey tonight. "He's not here."

Joanna pushed back her chair, alarmed. "What do you mean?"

"There's no need to be upset," Martha said. "He's the reason why I'm here. He needed some time away and I gave it to him."

"Time away from what?"

"You mean who," Hildie said.

Martha sent her a significant look then quietly said to Joanna, "He needs space."

"From me?"

"From a lot of things."

"And you let him leave without telling me?"

"He's a grown man."

"He's my son and I have a right to know what he's up to. Anything could happen!"

"Nothing will happen."

Joanna turned to Graham. "Who was that girl he was seeing? You must find her and—"

"She's already returned home," he said. "Alone. I saw them at the airport. He kissed her on the forehead like she was his sister. He didn't get on the plane."

"James is not the type to run off with a woman," Martha said.

"But the ring she wore..."

Martha slowly blinked. "She wore a special ring?"

"Yes," Joanna said, rubbing the back of her hand. "She had an emerald...and James pretended to know her—" She paused. "I'm probably making too much of it."

"There was a young girl he'd once corresponded with. They'd both been in the hospital at the same time, don't you remember?"

"No."

"Well," Martha said. "He told me they were good friends and he will miss her. He liked her but she didn't return his feelings. The breakup was painful."

Joanna looked relieved then fixed her expression to look sad. "My poor baby. I shouldn't have let him get serious about anyone."

"He's young. He'll recover, but he needs space right now. I loaned him to one of your brothers—"

"Which one?"

"For a couple of months," Martha continued, making it clear she didn't plan on being specific. "I think work will keep him properly occupied."

"I hope he doesn't overwork himself."

Martha nodded. "I'm sure when you see him again, he'll be a new man."

CHAPTER 27

Off the radar. James knew that wouldn't last forever, but it didn't matter. He'd won. She was his. No one could stop them now.

"Smile for the camera!"

James turned to his new father-in-law, who was motioning to them as he stood at the bottom of the Randall County courthouse steps. The day was bright and humid, as could be the case for Maryland in the summer, people rushed from the building to their cars to escape the heat.

Michelle sighed. "Dad, you've taken enough pictures."

Her youngest sister, Jessie, tugged on her dress and frowned. "This itches."

"Stay still," her mother scolded before she turned to Michelle and said, "You decide to rush this wedding. Let your father try to catch the moment."

"It's my fault," James said with regret.

Her mother smiled at him as if he'd offered her a trip around the world. "No, we are happy to welcome you to the family."

Michelle's middle sister Teresa beamed. "I knew this day

would happen. I knew it. I knew it. I knew it." While Jessie continued to tug on her dress and mumbled, "Did you really have to invite the Prestons to the reception?"

"Say cheese!" her father said.

Michelle turned to James looking a little embarrassed. "I'm sorry about all this."

James looked at Teresa, Jessie, and Mr. and Mrs. Clifton with affection. He'd only known them a few days but already felt like family. "Don't be. This is everything I'd ever hoped for." He turned to the camera and smiled.

How COULD a man look so happy on his wedding day? Michelle stared at their wedding picture, which sat on the mantelpiece of their new, fully furnished home. In the photo, James beamed as if he'd discovered the cure for cancer, won a trip around the world and a tiny island combined. And he looked...so young. Nothing like the brooding man she'd seen at the castle only months ago. At times, she forgot he was only twenty-five but staring at him now he looked like a young man with a bright future and she looked...

She was a beautiful bride, not in the normal sense, but somehow...maybe it was a trick of the lens, the way the sunlight caught her face, but she glowed. She remembered her brief hesitation only hours before having the photograph taken when she stood alone with her father in the hallway.

Michelle looked at her father amazed it was her wedding day. "Am I doing the right thing?"

"That's not a question I can answer for you."

"Do you think it's happening too fast?" she asked, wanting him to know she was still the sensible one. The one he could depend on. "I know I should have told you about him sooner and I know it's strange that his family isn't here and—"

"Do you want to marry him?"

Michelle took a deep breath and said without hesitation. "Yes."

Her father's face spread into a wide smile. "Then let your heart lead you down the aisle."

And she had and didn't regret a single moment.

Michelle heard James's footsteps behind her then felt his hand on her shoulder. "What are you doing?"

"Looking at us."

He lifted her up in his arms.

She gasped in surprise. "What are you doing?"

James spun her around. "I want you to look at me instead."

She wrapped her arms around his neck and laughed.

He stopped spinning, his eyes clinging to hers. "Do you like the house?"

"Yes," she said. She rested her head on his shoulder, liking the soft feel of his cotton shirt against her cheek and the scent of spiced tea. "I've told you that before."

"Happy?"

Michelle lifted her head, surprised by the question and saw a glint of uncertainty in his gaze. "No, I'm ecstatic." She kissed him with a heart full of love and he kissed her back with the same passion, neither of them knowing that their joy would last less than a year before the troubles began.

CHAPTER 28

They woke up to something pounding on the front door.

James rolled onto his back and mumbled. "What is that? A storm?"

Michelle grabbed her robe, more awake than he was. "Someone's at the door. It sounds urgent." The pounding stopped, replaced by the insistent ringing of the doorbell. She rushed barefoot to the door and swung it open.

Joanna pushed past her. "Where is my son?"

Michelle stumbled back too startled to speak. Silently watching as another man followed behind her. The same one she'd seen at the castle.

Joanna spun around to her, her long black cape swirling about her. "Where is he?'"

Michelle pointed. "He's upstairs. I can—"

Joanna took a menacing step towards her, her eyes cold. "Did you think we'd never find out? Did you think you could keep him all to yourself forever?"

"No, he said—"

"Hello, Mum."

Joanna turned to James as he came down the stairs. She held out her hands, frightened. "Careful. Careful you might fall. Why did you have to get a place with stairs?" She turned to Michelle. "Did he tell you about his accident when he was eight?"

"Six," James corrected.

"You know how dangerous they can be." She rushed over to him when he reached the bottom of the stairs. She touched his face. "You look pale."

He took a step back. "I feel fine."

Joanna reached for him again, cupping his face in her hands. She turned to Graham. "Doesn't he look pale?"

James pushed her hands away. "What do you want?"

"What do I want? You don't communicate for months—"

"I did communicate."

Joanna gestured to Michelle. "You didn't tell me about *this*. You disappear without an explanation to me, you marry in secret and you want to know what I *want*?"

James took her arm. "Sit down and let me explain."

Joanna pulled away from him. "There's nothing to explain. You're going to come home and get this farce annulled."

"Mum, sit down."

"We were going to tell everyone eventually," Michelle said, "but James—"

Joanna pinned her with a look. "Don't you dare blame him for this. Don't pretend you didn't persuade him. Coax him. I don't know how, but you did because I know what you are. You saw the money and—"

James stood in front of Michelle, blocking his mother's view. "Go back upstairs. I'll—"

"We should face this together." She took his hand. "I'm not afraid and she has a right to be angry."

I won't let her take that anger out on you.

I'm strong.

"What are you two whispering about?" Joanna demanded. "Is she pregnant?"

James spun around to her. "No, but—"

"Good, then we came just in time." Joanna wrapped her hand around James's arm, her nails seeming extra red against his brown skin. She looked at Michelle. "How much do you want?"

Enough to make you leave us alone. "I don't want anything," Michelle said, fighting to keep her voice polite. "I understand why you're upset but—"

"No, you don't understand."

"Honey, please go back to bed," James said, but this time his tone sounded tired. And when she looked at him she was alarmed to see he did look a little pale. "I'll sort this out."

She took his hand, she didn't know what was going on, but she felt the need to. "You're strong," she said in a low voice.

"Yes, go up to bed," Joanna said. "James and I need to talk alone."

Michelle kept hold of James's hand although she was suddenly starting to feel a little tired too. Her gaze went back to Joanna's hand. Could she be influencing him? If James had a talent, his mother might have one too. One similar to hers. Michelle dropped to the floor as if in a faint. James pulled away from his mother and rushed to her side. He lifted her to a sitting position. "Are you okay? What happened?"

"I don't know." She briefly looked at Joanna, and saw rage simmering in her gaze. And Michelle realized the older woman had a dangerous talent that she wasn't sure of yet. She would have to tread carefully.

Go back to bed, James silently told her.

No.

"It's probably low blood sugar," Michelle said aloud. She let him help her to her feet then took his hand and walked past the silent Graham who stood near the couch. "Let's sort this out like he said."

"What is there to sort out?" Joanna sat in front of them and looked at James. "We have to end this before it's too late."

"It's already too late," he said. "She's my wife."

"It's not too late to end things. Otherwise you'll only end up hurt."

"We love each other," Michelle said.

Joanna sniffed. "James doesn't love you. He's using you to hurt me. To get away from me. From the truth of his life."

James shook his head. "That doesn't make any sense."

"Yes, it does. Running won't change that any woman—"

"Michelle, doesn't need to hear this. She—"

"I know about his talent," Michelle said.

Graham spoke up. "Do you know about the cur—"

James turned sharply to him. "No." He looked at his mother. "And she doesn't need to."

Joanna looked at him stunned. "Have you gone completely mad?"

"I know what I'm doing."

"No, you don't." She pointed to Michelle. "And neither does she. You should have at least told her the truth!"

"She knows all that she needs to."

"About what?" Michelle said.

"You don't need to hear this," James said.

"The curse," Graham said.

Michelle frowned. "I don't think what he's able to do is a curse."

He frowned. "What?"

"She's not afraid," James said.

"Because she doesn't know everything."

"That's enough."

"She deserves to know the truth," his mother said. "You should have told her everything." She turned to Michelle. "Perhaps I was wrong about you. Maybe you are the victim of my son's silly rebellion." She shook her head in pity. "None of what he's told you is real. It's all in his mind."

"Mum."

"It's all an act. He's pretending because this is how he wants his life to be. Not how it really is."

He turned to Michelle. *Go upstairs!*

No.

Please.

No, I have to hear this.

"You're not the one to break it. No one can. Especially not a woman. And I'm not being sexist that's what the prophesy said."

James shot to his feet. "I said that's enough!"

Joanna leaned back and stared up at him. "Fine, then you tell her."

"Yes, tell me," Michelle urged him. "Tell me about the curse."

James looked up at the ceiling and sighed then sat back down. His eyes met hers. "You mean the one that says my wife will kill me?"

CHAPTER 29

Michelle stared at him, stunned. "Kill you?"

The corner of his mouth kicked up in a rueful grin. "Sounds ridiculous, doesn't it?"

Icy fear twisted her heart. No, it didn't sound ridiculous. It sounded awful. "Why didn't you tell me this before?"

"Would you have married me?"

"I don't know." Michelle shook her head at a loss. "I don't know anything right now."

"Now that you do know," Joanna said, "You understand what you must do."

James took Michelle's hand and stood. "Excuse us," he said to his mother then led Michelle to their large formal living room. He gently pushed her down on the grey couch then stood in front of her. "I've heard about this curse since I turned nine. I was told that I was never to marry. That that was my fate. My wife would kill me.

"As a child I didn't think much of it to be honest. I didn't care about getting married. And at that time there had been whispers that I wouldn't live long enough to worry about it anyway. When

I got older I was still in and out of doctors' offices, so much of the spare time I had, I used to work, to help the family business. I was fine. I wasn't convinced there was a woman out there for me until..." He held her gaze. "I don't know what came over me but the instant I noticed you at the castle, I knew I had a different future. I knew you were the one."

Michelle's brows shot up. "To kill you?"

James shook his head. "You're not going to kill me."

Michelle still couldn't believe what he'd told her and didn't like his cavalier attitude about it. A prophesy like that wasn't to be taken lightly. "Did the Seer say how you would die? How old you would be?"

"No, only that I'd be cut down in my prime but there were never any specifics."

"Has the Seer been right before?" His hesitation gave her the answer she needed. "How often?"

James sat down beside her. "Michelle—"

"Tell me."

He rubbed the back of his neck. "So far...ninety-five percent." He grinned. "So there's a five percent chance—"

Michelle frowned. "That's not funny."

"You don't believe in fate, remember? You told me that."

A chill entered her heart. "But you thought we'd meet again by fate and we did."

He held her hands in his. "I think our fate and the prophesy are two different things. I wouldn't have married you if I thought—"

Michelle pulled her hands away. "You should have told me. You should have given me a chance to..." She shook her head in dismay. "We didn't have to get married."

"And what about after I die? How will property and assets be handle and what about our children?"

"There are ways. We could have thought of something, come up with a plan."

"I wanted to marry you no matter the risk."

Michelle leaned forward, holding her head in her hands. "This is why nobody knew about us. Why you wanted to keep it all a secret."

"It wasn't a secret from everyone."

Michelle lifted her head. "What?"

"My grandmother knew. You passed the test for a reason. The Seer also said I had a chance at happiness with a special woman who wears an emerald ring. She believes, as I do, that the curse is broken. The moment we made love we were bound—you felt it too."

"Yes, but—"

James cupped her face in his hands, his deep voice resonant with meaning, his brown eyes shining with hope. "You will not kill me, Michelle. With you, I have a life."

CHAPTER 30

Joanna was pleased at the sight of James returning to the family room alone, but asked about Michelle anyway because she knew it was expected. "Where is she?"

"Having a lie down."

"She has to face that this marriage is now over."

James shrugged. "You know the Seer wasn't specific. Perhaps it's an *ex*-wife that kills me."

Joanna sent him a look. "Don't joke about it."

"What's done is done."

"Don't be stupid. You know this can't last."

"Mum, I'm happy. I've never felt better in my life and I haven't had any blackout incidents or...when I'm with her..." He shook his head in frustration. He looked up at Graham for a moment as if the other man could give him the words, then thought better of it and turned to his mother again. "I want this. I need this. I have to be with her."

Joanna tightened her lips. "Even when you know what will happen and—"

"We don't *know* anything. The future is still—"

"Your future has been predicted. You can only see the past not the future. You don't know anything about this woman. You're so young. You think you're in love but you're merely grateful. I blame myself. I should have exposed you to more people." She rubbed her hands together as a thought came to her. "This is what we'll do. Over the next year you'll meet other women—"

James shook his head. "No. I'm not leaving my *wife* and she's not leaving me."

"Have you had any episodes yet?"

"No. I just told you—"

"Not even small ones," Joanna insisted.

"Does she know about them?" Graham said, toying with his pinkie ring.

James sighed. "Nothing has happened."

"Yet."

"She's stronger than any Seer's words. A curse can be broken."

"Or it can come true."

James stood. "This is my home now. Either you accept it as it is or you don't."

Joanna sighed. "Are you truly happy?"

"Yes."

"Then you leave me no choice." She held open her arms in surrender. "I don't want to lose you."

James hugged her relieved. "Thanks," he said.

Soon after, Joanna showered them with gifts, hoping to show her change of heart. She gave them new bed linens, dining sets, clothes.

"Can't you tell her this is too much?" Michelle said when a

silk dress arrived for her as a gift for their one year anniversary.

James looked at the dress Michelle had draped over the couch. "It's her way of saying sorry." He stood behind her and wrapped his arms around her waist. "I can't wait to see you in it."

Michelle felt a little guilty for not feeling as eager. "She needs to stop doing this."

James gave her an affectionate squeeze then kissed her on the cheek. "Don't worry, it won't last much longer."

But more gifts came. And the more that came, the more James started to change. It was subtle at first, like the soft touch of autumn chilling the air and brushing color on the tips of leaves. That's when Michelle began to notice him not sleeping as soundly, then he started sleeping more. Soon he started tiring easily; stumbling over his words at times.

Then slowly over the following year a change came over his face. That expression she'd once seen at his London flat returning —a cruel, hungry look. It never stayed. It came quickly but then it was gone. She wasn't frightened of him, but of it. Whatever *it* was. It had taken over their house, she could feel it.

But when she invited family and friends over no one acted differently. Michelle thought perhaps the Winfields would notice something when James's cousin, Cory arrived with his parents and sisters. Cory was as incorrigible as ever, making them all laugh. Michelle saw that James got on well with his cousins and uncle, giving extra attention to his aunt Angela who seemed to stay away from sweets unless James offered them to her. Although Michelle sometimes caught Angela sending nervous looks at James when she saw him talking to her husband, when Michelle asked her if anything was wrong, Angela told her she was just impressed by how much the Winfields turned to James for advice then changed the subject.

No one sensed *it*. No one saw a change in James and many

times when he'd send her a smile over his laptop when he worked in the family room, or wink at her on the drive back from their beach house, or hold her in his arms at night on a surprise trip to Portugal, she wondered if she imagined it.

Had Joanna's visit made her paranoid? Filling her mind with reasons she'd have to hurt him? Have to protect herself?

She felt betrayed. He should have told her about the curse.

The curse. Why would anyone have to kill him? But as more days passed she knew. She knew there was something greater within him connected to his talent. Something he wasn't aware of. He'd always asked her if she was afraid of him. Did he know that she should be? Was he hiding something else?

But any time she thought to mention the curse she lost courage. He was happy and their life was good. It was all in her mind. However, when James would forget simple things she'd told him, or gaze at her with a look that wasn't his, she knew something was wrong. She didn't know who to talk to. She didn't want to tell her family for fear they would worry about her safety. Her father had told her that she was strong—that the emerald ring would bind love to her.

She had to believe that. It had to be Joanna's influence somehow. She asked James if she could donate some of the larger gifts Joanna had given them—an ornate mirror, an elegant crystal figurine, anything she felt could hold and harness energy—and he hadn't argued. But the darkness remained.

As another autumn turned to winter, and James stopped smiling as he used to, as the penetrating, brooding gaze lingered longer in his eyes, her fear grew and the prophecy loomed larger in her mind. *You will kill your husband.*

Kill.

Kill.

Kill.

CHAPTER 31

Michelle woke up with a cry on her lip as she felt a burning sensation on her back. She scrambled naked out of the bedroom, after a night of lovemaking, into the bathroom and switched on the lights. She turned her back to the mirror and saw claw marks on her back. Blood dripped down to the floor. She quickly grabbed a towel and cleaned it up. She had to clean it. Quickly. He couldn't see. Once she was finished, she jumped into the shower.

"A shower in the middle of the night?" James said, sliding the glass door aside. "You didn't think to wake me?"

She quickly spun around. Her eyes wide.

His smile fell. "What's wrong?"

"Nothing."

He glanced at the bloody rag in her hand. "What happened? Are you hurt?"

She opened her mouth then closed it. "James."

"What are you hiding from me?"

"It's...I'm fine."

He reached for her then froze and stared at the sight of the shower washing blood from his fingers. He didn't lift his gaze as he said in a low voice, "Turn around."

"James, please."

"Turn. Around."

She slowly did.

He swore.

She spun back to face him. "It's not your fault."

He stumbled out of the shower.

She quickly turned off the shower and followed him. "I'm sure it's nothing."

He glared at her. "Nothing?"

She grabbed a towel and wrapped it around herself, wincing as it touched her scars. "It's not your fault."

He shook his head. "You don't know that." He wrapped a towel around his waist and left the room.

She followed him. "I do. It's never happened before."

He sat on the bed. "We weren't married before."

"What does that mean?"

He shook his head again. "It means." He touched his forehead with trembling hands. "I've made a mistake."

"You're sorry you married me?"

"Yes, no...it's not that simple."

"Then explain it to me." She folded her arms. "What else are you hiding from me?"

"I didn't think I needed to hide. I thought it was over."

She sat down beside him. "What was over?"

"The curse. I thought...I thought our love had broken it but clearly..."

She took his hand. "It's not you. There's something in this house. Something dark. It followed you."

He hung his head. "I was afraid of that." He closed his eyes, his voice weary. "It's not the house." He turned to face her. "It's me. I have a dark power, the power of the beast."

"Beast? What beast?"

"I'm sure you've heard some version of the story of the cursed child touched with the blood of the beast."

"I've *never* heard of such a thing." Her father had been full of tales but nothing like this.

"I have," James said with a cynical laugh. "All my life. I was told 'In your bloodline there will be one who is sacrificed. He will carry darkness with him and will be killed by the one he loves and then the curse will be broken.' It seems my family angered a vengeful force many years ago."

"I don't believe this."

James held up his hand as if the blood was still there. "This is proof." He paused and looked at her. "Wait. You said you thought something dark was in the house. But you've never said anything to me before." His gaze sharpened. "How long have you been afraid?"

Michelle shook her head. "I wasn't afraid of you—"

"How long?"

It's been growing for years. "A few months."

James narrowed his eyes and for a moment she wondered if she'd shared her thoughts aloud.

"Have I hurt you before?"

Michelle took a deep breath relieved he hadn't sensed anything. "Never. And I don't think it's you. I'm sure there's another explanation."

"I can hurt people without realizing it. At night especially. It's not something I can always control. I'll have blackouts. This is why you'll eventually have to kill me."

"No, no I—"

"Don't lie to me, Michelle. I know I scared you that night at my flat."

She touched his arm, and said in a soft, soothing voice. "No, I was never afraid of you. I sensed something else in your flat that I didn't like. That night I was happy to be with you. I'm always happy to be with you. I'm safe with you."

A sour grin touched his lips."I'm afraid now that we're bonded that trick of yours doesn't work as effectively anymore. You can say I'm immune."

"You're not immune," Michelle continued in the same soothing tone. She wouldn't be tricked by the dark energy, she wouldn't give up on him. She knew she could reach him. "You're not cursed and you're not a beast."

James held her gaze for a long moment before he said in a soft, sad tone, "And if I am?"

"We fight it."

James shook his head. "We can't fight it. We can only kill it."

"Stop saying that. "

"It's all I know."

She patted her lap. "Lie down."

He hesitated.

Do it.

You think you can fight me?

I don't need to fight you. Now lie down.

He did.

She stroked his hair. Not to calm him, not as she would to calm a predator, but because he was the man she loved and she wanted to protect him. She felt the tension in him ease and said in a quiet voice, "We are together for a reason. I won't let you go. We can fight this together. Trust me."

CHAPTER 32

B ut he didn't.

A week later, Michelle returned home under a winter white sky and saw a black rental car in the driveway. When she stepped inside the house she saw suitcases in the foyer.

"What is going on?" she called out then stopped when Joanna approached her in the hall. "Oh, I didn't realize you were coming."

Joanna looked at Michelle with pity. James stood silently behind her. "I know what happened," she said.

"Nothing happened."

"Don't lie to yourself." She pointed to James. "Do you see how guilty he feels? Do you want this? He's only safe with me. Because one day you're going to be so frightened that you'll—"

Michelle covered her ears. "No."

James walked forward. "Mum, stop it."

Michelle stared at him, feeling betrayed again. *Why did you tell her?*

I had to.

No, you didn't.

She knows more than we both do.

Michelle headed for the stairs. "Let me get changed. There's no need to leave your things by the door. There's a room ready as always."

"We're not staying," Joanna said.

Michelle looked at her then at James confused. "I'm sorry?"

He took a deep breath. "I have to keep you safe."

"You're leaving me," Michelle said in a flat voice. Grief gripped her heart, but she was determined not to cry.

"Not for long. Just for a week or two to figure this out. Mum thinks she knows someone who can help."

Michelle took his arm and led him into another room before she turned and looked at him. "You were going to leave without telling me?"

"No, she came for a surprise visit and...and I told her. She convinced me—"

Michelle frowned. "That she was right?"

He rubbed his eyes. "No, but—"

"You don't have to leave." Her voice trembled but she held her tears in check. "Please don't leave me. Trust me. We can figure this out together."

He drew her into his arms and held her close. When he spoke his voice was tender, "I'm not leaving you."

"Yes, you are."

He pulled away and gazed down at her, pain shining in his eyes. "How can I stay with things the way they are?"

Her tone grew more eager, hearing the hesitation in his voice. "Trust me. Us."

James rested his forehead against hers. "Really?"

"Yes."

"And how am I supposed to keep you safe...from me?"

"I can talk to my father and—"

He lifted his head. "Once your family knows the truth about me it will change everything. Your family can't know about me. It's best this way. You know it too."

She didn't have an answer and for a moment the room faded away and they stood on a street corner, a double-decker bus passed by and she saw a mixed couple holding hands wearing bellbottoms. She could feel James wrapping her in another memory as she gazed at the man who was James but not him, dressed in a jaunty cap and shirt with a butterfly collar. He tenderly caressed her cheek and spoke. She didn't hear his words but felt his love and promises.

Michelle turned her face away and shook her head. "Stop it," she whispered. "I don't want to live someone else's memory. Let us have our own." She heard him sigh and the vision faded.

"I need you to know how I feel," he said.

She did, but it wasn't enough. He was still leaving her. She reached for his arm, but he moved away. "No, don't convince me to stay."

She let her hand fall to her side defeated. She didn't want to see him leave. Somehow she knew she would lose him.

And she was right.

THE PRESENT

CHAPTER 33

S he looked smaller.

Somehow she'd expected something different. Michelle looked at Martha, as the older woman sat behind the desk of her spacious Virginia office, surprised to see that she looked older. It had been less than seven years but Martha looked as if a decade had passed. She told herself that she didn't care. She couldn't afford to. She had to save her business and move on.

"I'm glad you could make it," Martha said.

Michelle sat down unimpressed. "Did I have a choice?"

Martha sighed. "I forgot you were never into small talk."

"Or peacock feathers," Michelle said referring to the first time they'd met. It had all been a show that hadn't meant anything and she was still annoyed with herself for being so gullible. She folded her arms. "What do you want?"

"I believe my letter made it clear. Would you like anything to drink?"

"Why am I here?"

She walked over to a table where two glasses sat. "I'm addicted to this new brand of sparkling water."

"I'm not thirsty."

She opened the bottle and poured it into the two glasses. "It has a hint of raspberry."

"And I hope to be back home by this evening."

Martha walked over to her and held out the glass. "You'll find it very refreshing."

Michelle glared at her, but when Martha didn't budge she relented and took the glass.

Satisfied, Martha retrieved her own glass and returned to her seat. "Hydration is very important. Keeps one from being too irritable."

Michelle tapped the side of her glass, the carbonated bubbles tickling her nose. She rested the glass on her lap. "Why did you want me to come here?"

"I wanted to see you again."

Michelle took a sip of the drink, annoyed that it was as refreshing as Martha had claimed, then shook her head. "I don't believe you."

"You've grown harder."

"What is this really about?"

"Moving on. It's time you completely cut ties with us and realize that he's not coming back."

"I'm not staying there because of him. It's where I've grown my business."

"You're determined to stay?"

"Yes."

"Fine. I want to see how good you are. I have a property on St. Clarine that's losing money. I want you to look it over for me, find the reason why it's doing so poorly and give me a report on changes I need to make to restore it. If I like what I hear we can come to an agreement. It shouldn't take more than a week or two."

James had once taken her to that Caribbean island. Like many others, it boasted exclusive waterfront property, white sandy beaches and coconuts the size of a man's head. She remembered drinking from one of them as she and James sat watching the sun set over the water. *Don't think of him.* "And if I do this then this ridiculous misunderstanding will go away?"

"Yes."

"Permanently?"

She nodded.

"Why me?"

"Scared you'll fail the same way you did with James?"

Michelle placed the glass on Martha's desk, smiling when she saw the older woman flinch because she didn't use a coaster. "I didn't fail him. He walked away."

Martha got a napkin and wiped the ring stain then placed the glass on a coaster. "And you let him. How come you're fighting harder to save your business than you did your marriage?"

Her words stung. It wasn't true. She'd thought he'd come back. She'd never thought he'd leave her for good.

"You haven't even once asked about him. To think I was foolish enough to believe that you loved him."

Yes, and I was foolish enough to believe he loved me. Her throat closed, tears threatened, but she wouldn't defend herself. She didn't care what they thought of her. Even if she told Martha everything, it wouldn't bring him back to her. "Are we through?"

Martha frowned. "You've become a cold woman."

"How's Joanna?"

Martha looked startled for a moment then regained her composure. "Do you have a message for her?"

"No, she already knows she won."

CHAPTER 34

I t was going to be a challenge.

Although the island of St. Clarine hadn't changed since Michelle's previous visit, getting to Martha's property was far from ideal. It was an almost forty minute trip that included a ferry and a half hour drive from the dock on an isolated dusty road.

"You sure you want to go there?" her taxi driver, a boisterous woman with yellow hair and skin the color of toffee, asked her for the second time.

Michelle typed some notes in her phone, pleased there still was a reception. "Yes."

"Because there are stories. A young woman like you went missing last year."

"Hmm." Michelle said, noncommittal. If there were ghost stories being bandied about that could also be one of the reasons the property wasn't doing well. The taxi driver told her about two other places closer to the center of town where she could stay, but soon gave up when Michelle made it clear she wasn't interested.

Now Michelle sat staring past the iron gates at the large

structure as the sound of rain pounded against the roof of the taxicab. She sighed. There was no reason for her to be there. From the outside it was clear why the property was losing money, she doubted it made any, no one in their right mind would stay there. The place looked haunted.

After such a daunting trek, it would take something spectacular to make visitors think it was worth their while. Right now it didn't even look worth a demolition. Michelle softly swore. Martha had given her an impossible task hoping she would fail. But she wouldn't.

A challenge. She'd given her a challenge and she'd come up with plan she couldn't refute.

"Here you are, Miss," the driver said.

"But we aren't there yet."

"Yes we are." The woman pointed to the gates. "The main house is just along this path here. Only a few yards. You won't miss it."

Michelle could tell the woman was nervous to drive past the gates. "I'll pay you extra to take me up there."

"It wouldn't be enough. Now if you want to stay at—"

"Never mind."

Seconds later Michelle pushed her way through the creaky iron gates, holding her suitcase over her head. She hurried up the curving drive, which had turned into a river of mud, towards the expansive building that had once been glorious with arched windows and columns, but now looked like a cruel, ugly parody of its former glory, with brush growing wildly around a marble fountain green with algae.

Michelle made it up the front steps, out of the rain and sighed, setting her suitcase down. She would look on the bright side. Beauty could be bought. The structure looked good. The

Winfields had the money and were willing to spend it, she'd help them do it then leave and get back to where she belonged.

Michelle knocked on the front door. She'd been told that the caretaker would assist her. She cast a glance behind her. She didn't know what he thought he was taking care of. The garden was a mess. She turned back to the door and saw peeling paint and a cracked trim that needed to be replaced. With such an unremarkable exterior she shuddered to think what the interior looked like.

She squeezed excess water from her jacket. What was taking so long? The air was warm so there was no chance of her catching a chill, but she was still sopping wet and wanted to change. She knocked again—harder. She'd given Martha the time when she'd arrived so things would be ready for her.

Before she could pull out her cell phone the door swung open.

"What do you want?" a man demanded.

Michelle couldn't reply. All words froze on her lips as she stared at him. James. James!

Or at least a man who looked like James if James had given up on shaving and had chosen to dress like a man who didn't have a penny to his name. He wore a yellow T-shirt with a tear near the shoulder, faded jeans and sandals. He was thinner than she'd remembered him but he still looked wonderfully magnificent and fierce.

"What are you doing here?" he asked her.

That was *her* question but she still couldn't speak. What was wrong with him? He stared directly at her but there was no recognition in his gaze. His eyes were the same dark, piercing brown but weren't as focused as she'd remembered them. And it was clear he didn't remember her.

She lowered her voice, to mask it from him. "Will you excuse me a moment?" she said, then turned and went along the veranda far enough away so that he couldn't hear. She pulled out her cell phone and dialed.

"You scheming, horrible old woman," she said once Martha picked up.

Martha giggled with delight. "You saw him then?"

"You lied to me."

"Have you seen him?"

"You said you needed help."

"Have you seen him?" she repeated. When Michelle didn't reply she said, "You see that he needs you and we didn't think you'd help him otherwise."

"He doesn't need help," Michelle said, finding her voice. "He needs a shave, some new clothes and—"

"It's bigger than that and you know it. Have you told him—?"

"I'm not telling him anything. He looks at me as if he doesn't know me. Did he lose his mind or something?"

"No, the truth is—"

Michelle shook her head. She couldn't let herself weaken. It had been a cruel trick, but whatever was wrong with James was none of her business now. She hadn't been able to help him in the past and she doubted that had changed. "I don't care. I'm taking the first ferry off this island the moment I get a chance."

Martha paused then said, "Do you still want the space in the Winfield building?"

Michelle heard the threat, but didn't care. She gazed out at the rain pounding the palm trees and soaking the sad looking fountain. "Not this much."

"Do you still want to have a business at all?"

A bigger threat. They could fulfill it. She'd worked too hard for them to snatch it away. "I will fight you."

"Yes, and lose gallantly. I'm not doing this to spite you. If I weren't desperate you would never have heard from us again."

"Is Joanna here too?"

Martha didn't reply.

"Where is she?"

Martha remained silent.

Michelle ran a hand through her wet hair in frustration. "What do you expect me to do?"

"James has wealth, the world at his feet, yet chooses to live this way. As if he didn't want to live anymore. All those years ago I trusted that you were the right woman for him. I still believe that."

"You were wrong."

"Prove it."

Michelle squeezed her eyes shut, feeling trapped. "Why are you doing this to me?" She opened her eyes and blinked back tears. "I reached out to you. A year after he left, I called you and left a message. More than once. I never heard back."

"This is my apology." She disconnected.

Michelle swore, resisting the urge to throw her cell phone in the mud. It wasn't fair. She took a deep breath. Calm. She had to be calm and focused. She put the cell phone away and lifted her head. They wouldn't defeat her. For the time being she was stuck until she came up with another plan. James didn't need to know who she was. She would play the role Martha had given her, as someone here to assess the property, then leave. Michelle returned to the front door ready to face this new challenge. This time when she raised her hand to knock the door opened.

"You're back," he said, but this time he didn't look at her, but rather at something over her shoulder.

She waved her hand in front of his face. "Yes."

He blinked as if he'd seen the movement, but didn't say anything about it. "Shame you have to leave again."

"I can't."

His eyes shifted to her face, but his gaze seemed vague. "Why not?"

"Didn't anyone tell you I was coming?"

"No."

I'm going to get you, Martha. I hate lies. "I'd like to come inside."

James folded his arms and to her annoyance she noticed the well-formed muscles under his T-shirt. "That's too bad."

"I didn't come all this way to be left standing in the rain."

He tilted his head as if listening. "Is it raining still? I thought it had stopped."

Michelle looked around her and, to her irritation, realized he was right. The sun had already begun peaking through the clouds, sparkling in the small puddles.

"How did you find this place?"

"I received instructions." She held out her cell phone and the email she'd printed. "Here you can read it."

"Actually no I can't." He turned away. "I'm afraid you've wasted your time. If you're quick you should be able to get on the next ferry out."

Actually no I can't. His words and the way he grasped at the door confirmed her suspicions. He couldn't see. That explained why he didn't recognize her. But when? How? Why had he stayed away? Why hadn't Martha told her? "I don't want to be here anymore than you want me to be here, but I don't have a choice," she said before he could close the door. "I only need to look around for two days minimum and then I'll be out of your hair. Understood?"

"Who sent you?"

"Your grandmother wanted me to look at the property."

He grimaced. "I should have guessed. There's no need. The property is mine."

"I don't care. Can we discuss this inside?"

His expression changed.

"What?"

"The way you said that...reminded me of someone." He shook his head. "Never mind. Come in then."

Michelle bit her lip and grabbed her suitcase. Maybe she should tell him who she was. Maybe she should find out what happened. She began to speak when James stepped back to let her pass.

The inside was worse. Much worse.

James held out his hand. "I'm assuming you have bags."

She gripped the handle, trying to process what was around her. "Just one. I can carry it myself. Thank you."

"Good."

Michelle stared around in horror. How could he live this way? Sight or no sight his other senses must have smelled the musky damp that clung to the peeling wallpaper and chipped paint, felt the threadbare furniture, worn rugs and table covered in dust. This is what he preferred? He preferred this derelict, isolated surrounding to living with her? Had it been so bad? It would have been better if she'd found another woman, a better life, anything than this shabby place. Tears of anger stung her eyes as her heart hardened.

She would make sure he never knew who she was. If he wanted this life, he could keep it. She would write her stupid report so she could return to the life she'd built for herself. She would not weaken as she once had. He was not wounded, she could not heal him. She'd learned her lesson the hard way. He'd developed the life he wanted and they were both better off alone.

Michelle swallowed away tears. No, what hurt the most was how much this place showed her how much she'd failed him. Love wasn't enough. Love would never be enough. He hadn't come back to her. At least with her business she could help people and they thanked her, she'd never been able to help him and she never would. Let him find someone else. Once she returned to the States she would start divorce proceedings and free them both since he didn't have the courage to do so.

James closed the front door, swallowing the room in darkness. She noticed a thin stream of light between the heavy drapes which covered the windows, keeping out the sun. She stumbled over to one and pushed it open. A cloud of dust surrounded her. She coughed and stepped back.

"Yes," he said in a dry tone. "I wouldn't do that."

"I didn't have a choice," she shot back. "It's too dark to see. Where are the lights?"

"Yes, right. Sorry. I hardly use them anymore." He hit a switch.

She felt contrite as she thought about his situation. She didn't mean her words to sound so cold, but she was tired and wet and angry. But despite her anger, every time she looked at him her heart moved. Her heart remembered loving him. Her heart wanted to know the reason he hadn't come back to her. Her heart needed to understand. Where was Joanna? Graham? Why was he alone here? Michelle took a step towards him, waving her hand in front of his face again.

This time he surprised her and mimicked the movement. "When the light is right I can see shadows," he said. "I see a semblance of shapes but nothing in detail."

"Oh," Michelle said feeling guilty for getting caught, but she was still curious. Her fingers itched to touch his face and she came to a decision. She would tell him who she was and why she was there and get some questions answered. She lifted her hand and began to say his name, but someone else beat her to it.

"James! I was only taking a nap. Why didn't you wake me?" a woman said from above. Michelle spun around, looked up at the landing and saw the only beautiful thing in the place. She watched as the woman floated down the stairs like a vision. The woman looked as if she'd been touched by God and raised from the earth in perfect proportion—rich, black hair cascaded down her back in twists, her face a delicate array of feminine features.

Michelle's heart shattered. This was the reason she'd feared. He wasn't alone. He'd found someone else. Of course he would have. A man like him, even without his sight, wouldn't stay alone for long. Joanna would make sure. Martha would have known that. Michelle bit her lip and took a hasty step back, her knees buckling from shock and despair.

James turned sharply to her as if sensing something was wrong. "Are you okay?"

"I'm fine," she said, moving away from his outstretched hand. To think she'd almost revealed herself. How foolish would she continue to be? He didn't deserve it. He'd chosen this life. What if he was working with this woman to fix up the place? What if she'd caught him on a bad day? She'd made up a story about him that wasn't true. He was okay. He didn't need her. "It's been a long journey and I'm wet and a little tired."

"You look a mess," the woman said, her brown eyes wide and full of kindness. Up closer she looked older, like a woman in her late-thirties and Michelle noticed makeup on her cheek that covered a bruise. Could James have hurt her? "Poor thing you must be starving too and he doesn't have the decency to offer you even a glass of water. Let me help you with your case. What's your name?"

"Mi-Margaret."

"I'm Delana. I'm so sorry you have to see the place like this, but we are thinking of repairs."

We. She made her claim clear. They were together and they were going to fix up the place just as she'd suspected. What game was Martha trying to play? "I'm sure it will be great."

"You're shaking. Come on. Let's get you into some dry clothes."

James took the case from Delana. "I'll show you the way."

Delana gaped at him. "But—"

"I know every inch of this place. I know where we can put her," he said making Michelle sound like an inconvenient piece of furniture. He grabbed the railing and started up the stairs. "Come on unless you want to get lost."

Michelle looked at Delana who only shrugged. She quickly took off her shoes. Although the place wasn't in the best condition, she didn't think it was good manners to track mud through it. She looked with regret at the muddy trail she'd left when she'd gone to the window to open the drapes.

"Leave them with me," Delana said, taking her shoes from her. "I'll get them cleaned up."

"Are you coming?" James called from the stairs.

"You'd better go," Delana said in a low voice then hurried away.

"Yes," Michelle said then followed him. She stared at his back—still as broad and wide as she remembered—as he walked to the second level. She could hear Joanna's worried voice, *Why stairs? You know how dangerous they can be.* What did Joanna think about all this? Where was she? Or had she chosen Delana to take her place? Perhaps she found her a better substitute.

"Your girlfriend's manners are better than yours," Michelle said.

James reached the top of the stairs and turned right before leading her down the hall.

"Matches her face." *Her beautiful face. Do you know she's beautiful?*

James continued walking, the wheels of her case rolling along the wood flooring as he pulled it behind him.

"I'll have to speak to her about her ideas for this place."

He paused and touched one door then continued walking.

"Please let her know that I'm not really hungry so she doesn't have to make a fuss."

James stopped and turned to her. "You can stay here." He opened the door, walked inside and left her suitcase by the bed. "It's the best I can think of so don't complain." He walked out and closed the door behind him.

Michelle stared at the door, trying not to be angered by his disinterest. He was a stranger to her now. She opened her suitcase and placed her clothes on the four poster bed. The room was sparse—under white sheets there appeared to be the shape of a chair and a small dresser—but at least there were only a few spider webs and with a good dusting and a small amount of water it would be clean.

She changed into a pair of dark linen slacks, a blue cotton blouse and sandals before she tested the mattress by pressing her hands against it. The bed squeaked but seemed solid. She gingerly sat down. It would work for the time being. Michelle looked at the closed door again, remembering James's silence and how he'd kept his back to her.

She'd never let him know she'd seen him. He'd never know she'd even been there. She would come up with a plan to beat Martha at this silly game then disappear from his life forever.

CHAPTER 35

"You didn't know she was coming?" Delana asked James as the sound of sizzling oil filled the kitchen as she fried breadfruit.

James sat with his feet up on the wooden table. It was not something he'd ever done before but he was free to do anything he wanted here. "Not a clue."

"Who is she?"

"I don't know. Someone my grandmother dug up to annoy me."

"Why would she do that?"

He shrugged. "I've stopped trying to figure her out years ago."

Delana tapped his foot and he reluctantly put his feet on the ground and sat up straight. He heard her set the plate on the table and smelled the coconut milk she'd used to soak them in before frying the slices. "She doesn't look like she wants to be here."

"That's good."

"But you should clean up a bit. I think you frighten her."

He rubbed his chin, pleased. "That's also good."

"She keeps staring at you funny."

He didn't care. He wasn't curious. What anyone thought of him didn't matter anymore.

"What if—"

"Don't worry yourself. She won't be staying long."

"You don't think she's here to replace me?"

He heard the fear in her voice. "You're safe. Nobody's going to replace you. Your place is here with me."

MICHELLE STARED at the table where Delana had prepared fried breadfruit and callaloo plus fresh papaya. The two women sat alone. Delana made her apologies for James saying he had work to do. Michelle knew it was a slight. He was making it clear he had better things to do than to entertain an uninvited guest.

"So how long have you been here?" Michelle asked, hoping her voice sounded neutral.

"A year. It may not look like much, but this is heaven to me."

Michelle took bite of her breadfruit. "What happened to your face?"

Delana's hand flew to her cheek. "Nothing."

"Did he do that to you?"

"James?" She shook her head. "Oh no. He saved me from...I have a good life."

Michelle saw the fear in her eyes. "Don't worry. I won't be in your way. I know what it's like to be a new couple."

Her eyebrows shot up. "A couple?" Delana threw her head back and laughed until tears filled her eyes. "Me and him?" She looked at Michelle's surprised expression and laughed harder.

"I'm sorry," Michelle said not understanding Delana's laughter. She didn't think it was *that* funny. "I thought you were together. You seem...close."

Delana sobered, wiping tears from her eyes. "What a thought. Never. It'd never happen."

Michelle felt her temper pricked. It wasn't that crazy an assumption. James may look rough, but he was still good looking and clever. Perhaps Delana thought him too young or didn't know his background and saw him as an eccentric foreigner. "Yes, I guess I was wrong."

Delana nodded. "And don't you try for him either. He's married."

She blinked. "He's married?" *Delana knew he was married?*

"Yes. That's the first thing he mentioned when I...well I...I met him a few years ago when I helped my older sister and her husband in the market. I remember him from all the other visitors because he was so distinctive and I noticed the older woman he was with. When he was alone, I flirted with him thinking it might go somewhere but then he lifted a necklace he saw for sale, mentioned something about wanting to buy it for his wife and that was it."

He mentioned he had a wife? Years ago? And Joanna had been with him?

Delana waved her hands. "But don't say anything. He refuses to talk about her or his marriage. It seems very painful. I once asked him about the necklace and he told me he never gave it to her. I think she passed on."

Michelle opened her mouth unable to believe what she was hearing. "She died?"

Delana nodded solemnly.

"He said that?"

"No, but he didn't have to." She leaned forward and lowered her voice. "I don't know everything, but I think he lost her the same time he lost his sight. I believe it happened after the attack."

"The attack?"

Delana frowned, suddenly looking anxious. "I thought you said his grandmother sent you."

"She did, but she only told me about the property."

"Strange she wouldn't tell you about the home invasion."

Michelle gripped her hand into a fist. Martha was full of secrets. She took a deep breath then reached over and touched Delana's hand. "You can tell me about it. The Winfields trust me."

Delana looked relieved. "You mustn't mention it to him."

"I won't."

"It happened in London about three years ago I think. Two men surprised him when he was alone in his flat. Beat him so bad...He was briefly in a coma. When he was well enough his family transferred him to an exclusive retreat out here on the island. I guess to get him as faraway from the memory of it all as they could.

"At that time I used to work at the retreat's registry office. Rich people from all over the world come with their flashy clothes and noses in the air, but I remembered him from the market and he was different than the rest. Always very kind, but even though he had plenty of visitors he seemed lonely and sad. He left when he was strong enough. When I needed a place to stay, he let me come here."

Michelle knew Delana was leaving out part of her story. This place was too far out of town for her to have stumbled upon it. The island wasn't *that* small. There was more to the story than she let on, but she'd wait until later to find out more.

But at least she knew they weren't together. He was married. He still said he was married. *Don't make too much of it,* a little voice said. *He still didn't come back to you. He preferred to be with her than with you.*

Two days. That was the deadline she'd give herself. Michelle sat on her bed and took out her laptop, prepared to play the role Martha had given her. She opened up her calendar. This evening she'd do a cursory review of the rooms and main level. She wouldn't work too diligently since she knew her effort wouldn't amount to much. Tomorrow, when the ground was dry, she'd take pictures of the exterior. The following day she'd put together her report and then send it.

The next hour, Michelle walked around and made notes, her mind bursting with ideas and possibilities. The property could be many things. A retreat, a hotel, a gallery. She walked out onto the veranda. She paused when she saw James sitting on the steps, then decided to ignore him and continue her assessment.

"Come and tell me something," he said.

She walked over to him. "What?"

He stood up and made a sweeping motion with his hands. "How's the view?"

There wasn't much to say, but she didn't want to mention the fountain and the iron gate. "In the distance, to my right, through the trees, I can see a bit of blue of the sea and the sun is slowly descending in an orange haze."

He nodded and waited. "That's it?"

"Yes."

A soft, amused smile spread over his lips. "You won't be able to sell the place with a description like that."

"My job isn't to sell anything only to come up with suggestions on how to improve or restore the property to make it profitable."

"I see." He shoved his hands in his pockets. "I'm sorry my

grandmother brought you into this ridiculous family issue. Make sure you're properly compensated."

"Hmm," Michelle said touched by the kindness in his tone. He sounded like the considerate James she remembered.

"You're very...quiet. I'm not used to it. Most people like to talk my ear off. Delana can't seem to stop at times."

"Yes, she does like to talk a lot," Michelle said, studying his face. "Especially about your wife."

Surprise then pain crossed his features before it was covered by a neutral expression. "She likes to talk about a lot of things she doesn't fully know."

"I'm sorry about your loss. She told me about your wife's passing."

He didn't move, keeping his profile to her. He didn't reply. Was that really pain she'd seen or guilt or something else entirely?

"Your grandmother—"

James spun to her, fastened his hand around her neck and shoved her against a column.

"Should not have sent you here," he ground out between his teeth. "Do you pity me? Do you see a pathetic, blind, broken man?"

"No," Michelle managed in a hoarse whisper, surprised by the strength of his grip.

"You are going to leave early tomorrow morning and never return. Understood? Blame me. Tell her I scared you." He put his face closer to hers, his breath warm against her face. "And don't be fooled, I *can* be scary." *You don't want to stay here. You want to go home as fast as you can.* The words entered her mind and it took her a moment to realize that they hadn't come from her, but from him. She had to be careful not to answer back although she was tempted to. She had to resist the urge to touch him and try a little persuasion of her own. She was stronger now. Would it work when it hadn't in the past? But she kept her arms by her side. He would not convince her to leave. She would never mistake the sound of his voice as her thoughts no matter how clever he was. He could not frighten her. But she licked her lips and trembled as if she were.

Satisfied, James abruptly released her and stormed inside, slamming the door.

Michelle grabbed her throat and sunk to the ground. She had to be careful not to push him too far. He hadn't hurt her, but the power of his rage had stunned her. Rage. Against what? Against whom? Why James? Why?

She stared out at the mango trees, wiping away a tear. She would not fall in love with him again. That would be foolish and the years had taught her the consequences of that. But why did her heart have to betray her? Why him? Why did it not beat like this for any other man? He wasn't even as he had been before and yet...and yet he hadn't changed at all. That shy smile, the way he cocked his head while listening. Why did he pretend to care? That had been his biggest deception. She truly thought he'd cared about her. She wouldn't have fallen for him so completely if she hadn't believed that. And she also thought, stupidly, arrogantly, that she could help him. That she was what he needed. Her father's foolish stories had set her up for disappointment, but her father was gone and so was any lasting hope that she could be with James. Two more days and she'd give Martha what she wanted and prove that she wasn't what the older woman wanted her to be. Because the darkness wasn't here. She didn't feel it in the house, sense it in his face. He was angry by her presence there and had only tried to scare her. But he was free. He'd be freed without her. In two days she'd leave this place, get off this island and bury her past forever.

Delana rushed out the door. "What happened? James is in such a state."

Michelle stood and shook her head in regret. "It's my fault. I upset him."

"How?"

"I suggested some changes he didn't want." She gathered up her notebook and pen, which she'd dropped. "I won't make that mistake again."

CHAPTER 36

Delana watched Margaret go back inside. She was a strange woman. Delana started to follow wondering what she should fix for dinner when her cell phone rang. Her heart tightened. It was him and he'd want a report.

"How are things?" he asked in a low voice.

She looked around to make sure she was alone then crept around the corner. "Fine."

"What happened?"

She sighed. He always seemed to know when something was wrong. "Some woman came today."

"Who?"

He didn't sound angry, only curious. That was a good sign. "Some woman to look over the property I think. James isn't happy about it."

He sounded amused. "No, he wouldn't be. How long is she staying?"

"Not long by the looks of things. James said his grandmother sent her."

He suddenly swore. "What's her name?"

"Margaret. I didn't get a surname."

"What does she look like?"

"Professional. I guess."

"Pretty?"

Not really. "Uh...she's okay."

He swore again.

Delana became more alert. She didn't want him angry. He was awful when he was angry.

"What do you want me to do?"

"Just wait."

CHAPTER 37

Michelle entered the house and saw James sitting alone in one of the worn, sagging chairs. He held his head down and looked nothing like the man who had just threatened her. He looked sad and dejected.

She headed for the stairs. She'd dealt with him enough for one day.

I need you.

She stopped halfway up the stairs as his words entered her mind. The same cruel words he'd sent her weeks ago. She'd fallen for Martha's trap, she wouldn't fall for his. She was cutting ties with the Winfields forever. She continued up the stairs. *No, you don't, you selfish bastard.*

Michelle?

She stiffened then spun around. Oh no! She hadn't meant to say that to him. They were close now, she should have been more guarded. Michelle looked at him, her heart pounding. Would he suspect anything?

His head remained lowered, but his posture had changed. It had become more focused and alert. *Michelle?*

She bit her lip. *Where are you?*

When he covered his face in misery and said *England* her eyes filled with tears feeling the weight of his lie. *I'm traveling to Thailand soon.*

You sound busy.

I am.

She sat down on the stairs. *Come back.*

No.

Why not?

He shook his head. *I just can't.*

She stood. *Then you don't need me.*

Michelle? Michelle?

She bit her lip fighting the urge to respond.

Michelle? Michelle? Please. Don't go yet. He lifted his head as if that would help him hear her reply. *I'm sorry.* When he was met with silence she watched his shoulders sag. The beaten posture returning. What did he want from her? His lie about being in England didn't matter, she wanted to comfort him. To be with him again. She began to race down the stairs, but stopped when Delana walked through the door and saw him. She quickly went to his side and hugged him.

He let her, resting his head on her chest. She saw the bond there. She was not someone he would push away. He wouldn't leave her. And in the dying light she saw what she'd truly feared —beauty had tamed the beast. Despite the damp, derelict surroundings this beautiful woman had brought James peace. No dark energy swirled around him, he had strength. Their silent connection didn't matter. Their love was an illusion. Her father had lied to her. She should never have followed her heart. Michelle angrily wiped away her tears and went to her bedroom.

～

SHE'D NEVER SEEN him like this and it worried her. Delana stroked James's cheeks feeling the wetness of his tears. She'd never seen him cry before. "What happened? What did she say to you?"

He shook his head. "It wasn't her. I felt her. I heard her."

"Who?"

"My wife." Instead of sounding sad, he sounded relieved, amazed.

She would leave the poor man to his delusions. She shouldn't have trusted that Margaret woman. She did talk too much sometimes. Mentioning his wife hadn't been smart. That woman...she did have a scheming glint in her eyes. Perhaps when she'd been on the phone she should have told him as well. But she would keep James safe. She wouldn't let someone like Margaret hurt him.

"I didn't think it was possible," James said. "And I don't know how I did it. But she heard me and responded."

She took his hand. "Let me get you something to eat."

"And you think I'm crazy," he said with a rueful grin.

"No."

He drew away. "I'm okay now." He rubbed his chin. "I probably should shave."

"You do look fierce."

"I think I'll change too." He stood.

She was glad to see him looking brighter, even if it was for the wrong reasons.

"Are you sure it wasn't Margaret who upset you? I could have a word."

"I'm sure." He paused, then said in a pointed voice. "What does Margaret look like?"

Delana opened her mouth to describe Margaret's dark skin and rather plain looks then remembered how her lover had responded to her description on the phone. Perhaps she was trouble. James had been upset enough. She didn't want to cause him anymore pain. "Honey skin. Very attractive with wide eyes."

He appeared disappointed. "Oh. Well, I'll change anyway."

"And shave. By the time you come down I'll have prepared something delicious."

CHAPTER 38

She heard them laughing together. Michelle had crept down to the kitchen, lured by the scent of spicy chicken and rice. Her stomach growled but she wouldn't join them, she knew her presence would end their private joy and she didn't want to disturb them. She'd sneak into the kitchen later.

She remembered when she and James used to laugh together. How he'd teased her about covering up Cory's inadequacies and she'd told him about the jar of sweets. She remembered the way the setting sun painted her London flat in pale pink and purple as she read her business ideas to him. She'd thought it strange the way he would listen, never realizing how lonely she'd feel without him. Without his support and unwavering belief in her. The slight smile on his face he'd have anytime she started to doubt herself. When had he stopped believing in her? How had Delana broken the curse?

Or perhaps *she* was the danger. The prophesy had said his wife would kill him. Perhaps this was Martha's way to tell her to move on. To let go. To make him let go. He was still clinging to her and that was making him suffer. Michelle stuck her head around the corner. Delana's back was to her; James facing her, looking happy. He looked much better than before—clean shaven, dressed in a tailored green shirt. More like the James of the past. Did Delana's embrace encourage that change?

Although he'd reached out to her in his thoughts, he had to see that there was no chance for them to be together. He was to build his life with Delana now. Although Delana had said there was nothing between them perhaps she'd lied and secretly wanted more. As Michelle turned away a bitter jealousy stirred inside her. She rested against the wall and looked down at her ring. *I get it now. I get it.* She would conquer this pain. In this tale, she was the witch—the outsider—it was her duty to triumph over her own dark feelings. The ring was a healing stone. A love stone. She would help him to be with his true love and free them both.

THAT NIGHT, Michelle knew what she needed to do. She would connect with James one last time and convince him of what he must do. She waited for him to settle into bed then crept to his room, relieved that he and Delana slept apart. Fortunately, he left his door partially open allowing her to slip inside without a sound.

I'm here. She took hold of his hand, capturing his thoughts. *You're dreaming. It's all a dream. A final dream of me and you.*

He didn't move. *Final?*

Yes.

James's hand tightened around hers. His palm hot, his grip strong. *Then don't leave.*

She pressed her lips to his hand. *I can't stay long.*

You can stay the night.

James—

"Let me hear your voice," he said out loud.

Michelle closed her eyes. He was asking too much. She wasn't ready to talk to him as herself yet.

Please darling. Say my name.

Darling. How she'd missed him calling her that, making her feel precious to him. She was once precious to him and soon she wouldn't be any longer. Her throat tightened, but she managed to say his name. "James."

He shook his head, his brows furrowed. "You feel so close. Why do you feel so close?" He sat up and his hand slid up her arm. "It's like you're right here. You're here with me." He pressed his hand against her cheek. "Darling, it's you."

She took a deep breath, trying to steady her heart. "For a while. This dream only lasts for a while."

James pulled her into his arms, embracing her. She could feel his heart racing. "I don't want to wake up."

"Why did you leave me?"

"You know why." His hand fumbled to her mouth. "Shh...no questions. You're here. That's all that matters." He bent his head and kissed her—slowly, deeply, tenderly. Like a man in love. It was too much to bear.

She drew away from him, but kept her hand on his arm and said in a soft, steady voice, "You're where you're meant to be. The darkness is gone. You're not a beast and you...you don't love me anymore. You loved what we had. The memory of our time together that's all. But don't let that shut her out. You want Delana. You need Delana and she needs you."

His warm lips descended to her neck and he left a trail of kisses there. "I need you," he said, his voice low.

She felt her body respond to him. She licked her lips as she felt his hand slide under her nightshirt. "Yo-you need Delana so much. You're starting to forget all about me."

"Never," he said in a low growl and in one motion she was in his arms, his mouth covering hers with a kiss that left her breathless. She closed her eyes, letting her sensations swirl. Her body craved his touch. She deepened the kiss, arching her body into his, growing damp with longing.

She touched his cheek, his smooth cheek. Michelle paused. When she'd first arrived, his face hadn't been shaven. He'd shaved and changed for Delana. What was she doing? She was doing it all wrong and Martha would punish her for it. But she'd tried. He didn't seem to be affected by what she was saying. Why wasn't it working? Had she lost all power over him? She sensed that he was blocking her somehow. She pushed him away and scrambled to her feet. "No, I have to go."

"Wait. Stay a little longer."

She stepped back to stay out of reach. "No, I can't. Be happy."

He fumbled through the air searching for her. "Michelle, love—"

Goodbye.

James shot out of bed, but his foot got caught in the sheets and he fell to the ground with a thud. Michelle covered her mouth not to cry out. She gripped her hand into a fist not to run to him. It was time for this make-believe to end. She crept to the door, stepped outside then knocked on the door. "Is everything alright?" she asked, using her other voice. She walked into the room. "Are you okay?" She touched her chest, trying to sound a little breathless as if she'd run there.

"I'm fine," James grumbled, lifting himself off the ground.

"I heard a thud."

"That was me." He got back into bed then paused. "You got here fast."

Yes, she had. She had to remember how astute he was.

"I couldn't sleep. I was walking the hall when I heard you."

"Go to bed. I'm fine."

But he didn't look fine. He looked shaken. Sad. A little lost. He gripped the bed sheets, his hand trembling. And she realized she'd gone too far. Not only had he thought he'd heard from her but he'd fallen and she knew that was scary for anyone, especially someone with limited vision. She bit her lip feeling guilty. How could it have all gone so wrong? She'd wanted to free him not hurt him. She hurried out of the room blinded by tears. She'd failed him again.

Michelle returned to her bedroom and fell on her bed. She buried her face in her pillow and cried. She was alone. Desperately and horribly alone. Her love wasn't enough and neither was her sacrifice. Now she could lose her business and end up with nothing. She pounded her pillow with her fist. Why had her father given her false hope? Told her that she was strong, special? Why had James told her that she'd be his always? Why had she believed him?

Michelle cried until she felt weak then she turned on her back and stared up at the ceiling. She gazed up at the darkness gaining a new resolve. She would not be broken by this. *You've become a hard woman*, that's what Martha had said. Yes, hard and cold. That's what she needed to be. That's how Joanna had defeated her. How the Winfields had won. She would not be manipulated. She would leave tomorrow. She'd face whatever threat Martha delivered.

She closed her eyes and as she drifted off to sleep, she heard his voice. *Michelle? Michelle, I'm sorry.*

James couldn't sleep. His heart wouldn't stop racing. He'd held her again, heard her voice. Michelle. His darling Michelle. How could a dream feel so real? He'd connected with her twice. Or had it all been the vain imaginations of a dying man?

There was no medical reason for it. He just knew. He knew bonding with her had been a risk. Now, every year without her, shortened his days because he needed her. He needed her as he had the first time they met. She balanced him. Kept him from the edge, now there was nothing to keep him from it. And it kept calling. Not the darkness, the abyss. A crawling, aching emptiness that grew wider inside him each passing year.

This year he felt the end coming sooner. She was not only his other half, she was his heart and his body no longer wanted to live without it. He merely existed. But as he felt his energy force waning, he thought of her, dreamed of being with her one last time. Perhaps this had all been a wish fulfilled. Maybe he could travel to the States and visit her one last time.

Don't be selfish, she's still in danger. He sighed, yes that was why he had to stay away. He hadn't been cured. He'd gotten close, he thought, when he'd made an appointment with a top crystal and energy specialist, but before he could go he'd gotten attacked and his world had turned into shapes and shadows.

Shadows. One day that was all he would be to her—the shadow of a memory.

"YOU'RE LEAVING?" Delana asked Michelle, as Michelle carried her suitcase down the stairs.

"Yes, I'm sorry I bothered you."

"No bother. Would you like something to eat?"

Michelle hesitated. She knew she had quite a trek back. She had another hour before the taxi service was available and it was the only option on the island. It would be a long day so she should start out on a full stomach. "If it's not too much trouble."

"Not at all." She disappeared down the hall.

"You're up early," James said behind her.

"After a quick breakfast I'm leaving."

He nodded and headed in the same direction Delana had gone. He brushed past her then paused and grabbed her arm. There was an urgency in his movements and the expression on his face made her heart race. His hands raced up her arms then touched her face. She drew back but she was too late. He knew.

"No, it can't be," he breathed.

She didn't dare reply. Perhaps if she didn't he would doubt himself and let the moment pass.

In a frenzy his hands flew to her hands, then her arms, her face then her arms again. "Am I dreaming?"

She opened her mouth to say 'yes' he was, but Delana came

into the room and said, "What's wrong? Margaret, why are you crying?"

Michelle crumpled to the ground, covered her face and wept. She hadn't been able to escape without him knowing.

James knelt down and gathered her in his arms. He didn't speak, he only held her.

"What happened? What's going on?" Delana asked.

James held her tighter, his voice deep with emotion. "My wife...found me."

"But I thought—"

"Breakfast will burn."

Delana got the hint and left them.

Michelle stopped crying, but didn't lift her head and for a long moment she didn't move and he held her. They sat in silence. Finally Michelle said in a weary voice, "Aren't you going to tell me to get out? Tell me that you don't want me here? That I'm better off without you?"

James sighed, but didn't speak.

"Go on. I've felt it every moment since I've arrived. But you don't have to say the words. I know. I look around me and I know how you feel about me. I know that you'd prefer to live isolated on an island in this ugly house just to keep me safe. I know that you never planned to come back to me."

"Last night was you. It wasn't a dream."

"You're not listening."

"I'm not going crazy. You're really here."

"James. Let me go."

"Not yet."

"You don't need me. The darkness is gone."

"The darkness is real," he said in a deep tone.

"Not with her."

James released her. "What are you talking about?"

Michelle stood then reluctantly held her hand out to help him up. It took her a second before she realized her didn't see it. She took his arm and led him to the couch. "The energy in your London flat, the energy that...that seeped into our home. It's not here and I think it's because of her."

"I know." He swallowed. "I never wanted this. I'm sorry."

To hear him say it shook her to her core. Part of her wanted him to deny it. To give her another explanation. But now she knew the truth. He'd found someone else to heal him. "Then why did you say you needed me?"

He rested his head back and closed his eyes, tired. "Because I still love you."

"But we can't be together," Michelle said in a flat tone, admitting a truth that hurt her.

He shook his head. "No."

That's what Martha wanted them both to face. "I guess it's goodbye then. A divorce won't be difficult. I'll—"

James covered her hand, but didn't open his eyes. "Give me one more night."

"I don't think I should."

He tightened his hold. "Please."

Michelle touched his cheek. "You look tired. You didn't look this tired yesterday."

A secret smile touched his mouth. "That's because I couldn't sleep after you visited me last night."

"Oh." That seemed like a plausible reason, but she sensed something else. He looked as if he was being drained. Was that because of her? Was she that bad for him?

"Please stay," he said in a soft voice as he drifted off to sleep. "Just one more night. That's all I ask."

Michelle bit her lip. One more night. She wanted it as much

as he did. Then they'd part forever. "Okay." She took his hand. "You cannot fall asleep here. Let me take you to bed."

He let her help him to his feet then pulled her close. "No, you don't have to. I'm not an invalid." He kissed her—softly, tenderly—then turned and headed for the stairs. "Go eat breakfast. I'll join you later."

Michelle followed him, watching how he gripped the railing, his measured steps. His movement seemed labored. *Stairs can be dangerous,* Joanna had said.

"You don't have to help me."

She took his arm and draped it over her shoulders. "I want to." She slid her arm around his waist, bringing him closer. "And you want me to. You like how it feels."

He chuckled. "I won't argue with that."

She helped him into bed then turned to leave.

James sat up. "Remember—"

She gently forced him back down. "Don't worry. I'm not going anywhere." She saw his satisfied expression as he fell asleep and smiled. But her smile disappeared as she left his bedroom. There was something wrong. Something different about today than yesterday. Something different about him and even this house. There was no chance of them being together because she felt the darkness returning.

CHAPTER 40

His wife! Wasn't that amazing? And all this time she'd thought she was dead.

Delana stood near the counter and beat some eggs with a whisk. She shook her head. That Margaret woman really was a sneaky one. Of course, last night, she'd found out that wasn't her real name when she'd gotten a chance to go through her wallet. She hadn't liked the idea at first, but her honey had asked her to and she couldn't refuse him.

Michelle Clifton. That was her real name. She definitely wasn't the kind of woman she would have pictured James with. But the look on his face was priceless. He'd looked so relieved and happy. She didn't know whether to feel glad for him or not. Because now that James's wife had returned what would happen to her? What would she do now?

She set the bowl down and pulled out her cell phone. Her honey would know what to do. He always did. She smiled remembering how he'd surprised her last night. He'd snuck into her room and met her holding flowers. It was easy for him to slip into the house undetected. It was how their relationship had always been. No one knew about it. She found it thrilling, except when he got angry. But that wasn't too often. He was a good man. And one day he'd take her away from this island. That's what he'd promised her and she knew he had enough money to do it.

She called him. "I found out who she is. She's his wife."

He didn't sound impressed. "Where are they now?"

"In the living room," Delana said disappointed by his lack of enthusiasm. "I'm making breakfast."

"Good. This is what I want you to do..."

SHE SEEMED JUMPY, agitated. Michelle watched Delana drop a knife she'd used to butter toast. It was the second time she'd done it.

"Do you want me to help you?"

Delana picked up the knife and tossed it in the sink. "I'm fine." She placed a breakfast plate piled with an egg and spinach mix, toast and melon cubes in front of her.

"Looks delicious."

Delana turned away.

Michelle lifted her fork."I apologize."

"What for?"

She scooped up her eggs. "For deceiving you."

Delana shrugged, keeping her back to her. "It's not my business."

"You don't have to worry. I'm still not staying."

Delana spun around, startled. "Why not?"

The look on Delana's face told Michelle what she needed to know. Delana had been worried. She had feelings for James. "It would never work between James and me. We're getting a divorce. You can think of this visit as my final goodbye. I'll leave tomorrow."

Delana snatched Michelle's fork before she could bring it to her mouth, along with Michelle's plate. She dumped the egg and spinach mix in the trash bin.

"I think the eggs are off," she said when Michelle stared at her openmouthed. "Let me see what else we have."

"Okay," Michelle said. The eggs seemed fine to her and she thought her leaving would make Delana happy, but she seemed even more agitated than before.

DELANA THREW her clothes into her suitcase. He was going to be so angry when he found out, but she couldn't do what he'd asked. She'd done everything else, but his last request had gone too far. Once she was away she'd explain. He always needed time to calm down. When he wasn't angry then he would listen and realize she was right. Leaving would be easy. Michelle had gone for a walk and James was still sleeping. They wouldn't notice she'd left until later.

Delana zipped her bag closed then turned to the door. She swallowed a gasp when she saw Him standing there. He moved silently like a mist into the room.

He looked at her bag. "What are you doing?"

Delana set her bag on the ground. He didn't look angry. That was good. "I was cleaning out some things." She wrapped her arms around his neck and smiled at him. "You got here fast. Good to see you." She kissed him.

He didn't respond, but he didn't move away. "Did you do what I asked?"

Delana flashed a bright smile. "I didn't see the need." When he narrowed his eyes she started to speak quickly. "She's leaving tomorrow. She said they're getting a divorce."

"And you believe that?"

"Why wouldn't I?"

"I told you what to do."

"I know."

He removed her arms from around his neck. "And you disobeyed me."

Her body started to shake. Oh God he was angry. He had that look. She touched his cheek with light fingers. "I did it for us."

He trailed a finger along her jaw, a soft smile on his lips. "For us?"

"Yes."

"I'm going to give you another chance. This time you're going to do exactly what I tell you."

"Okay. I only thought it was a risk to—"

The first blow knocked her to the ground.

Delana held up her hands and stared up at him in terror. "I'm sorry."

"Good."

The second blow knocked out a tooth. She tasted blood in her mouth. "No...Please..."

The third blow knocked her out completely.

CHAPTER 41

He felt a presence.

James got out of bed and rubbed his sore hand. In his dream, he'd been fighting a shadow. He must have struck his bed in the process. He shook out his stinging hand and left his room. At least he didn't feel tired anymore and tonight he would be with Michelle.

But what was that strange feeling? The house felt empty but he sensed it wasn't. "Michelle?"

An eerie silence greeted him.

He walked to her bedroom and knocked on the door. "Michelle? Michelle, are you here?" He opened the door and made his way over to the bed in case she was sleeping. But the bed was as empty as the room.

But he still sensed a presence. Something was wrong. *Michelle?* he silently called to her. Maybe Delana could help him. He knocked then entered Delana's room and stumbled over something. Large, soft. Like a body. He fell to his knees, his hands sweeping over the form. Definitely a person. Motionless. Although frantic urgency seized him, he had to be gentle. He felt for a pulse, brushing aside her braids to get to her neck. By her hair he knew it was Delana. She was alive. He cradled her head and touched her face. A wet, sticky substance covered it. Blood. He could tell by the smell.

She moaned and started to sit up.

"Careful. It's okay, I'm here."

She froze then screamed.

He jerked back. "It's okay. You're safe."

She backed away from him. "Get away from me!"

She was in a state of shock. He held out his hands to show he wasn't a threat. "Shh...it's alright."

James heard footsteps racing down the hall. He heard them stop in the doorway then come rushing forward. "What happened?" Michelle asked.

James stood and shook his head. "I don't know. I found her like this."

"Get him away from me," Delana said.

He heard Michelle's voice soften. "Tell me what happened."

"James attacked me."

Stark, vivid fear coursed up his spine.

"What?" Michelle said.

"I don't know why," Delana said in a tearful voice. "He went into a rage and did this to me."

James stumbled back, covering his sore hand. "It's happening again."

"Quiet," Michelle said. "Delana, are you sure it was James?"

"Yes...Stay away! Don't touch me."

James heard Michelle halt. "Okay," she said. "But we need to get you to a doctor."

"There's a car she uses to get to town," James said.

"I'll take her. You wait here."

Michelle stole a glance at Delana as she sat curled in the passenger seat of the car like a scared creature. "Tell me what happened."

Delana closed her eyes and fiercely shook her head. "I don't want to talk about it."

"You're positive James—"

Delana glared at her."You asked me that before. I know what he did. You weren't there." She turned to the window. "I know why he left you now."

Michelle gripped the steering wheel and focused on the two lane road ahead. It didn't make sense for James to attack Delana all of a sudden. *But you felt the darkness,* a voice said. It was her fault for coming there. James's life had been fine until her arrival.

By the time she'd gotten Delana registered at the hospital and returned to the house, evening was setting in.

James met her at the door, blocking her entrance. "How is she?"

"Shaken. She'll live."

He frowned, his voice tense. "You shouldn't have come back here." He held out her suitcase. "I've packed your things."

Michelle pushed past him and walked into the house. "You didn't do this."

"You don't know that."

"Let me see your hand."

He sighed. "Michelle."

She took his hand and looked at the swollen knuckles. "Where's your First Aid kit?"

James pulled his hand away. "You're leaving here tonight."

"No, I'm not." She took her suitcase and headed for the stairs.

He grabbed her arm, stopping her. "Get out of here. It's happening again and I...I can't protect you."

"You didn't do this."

"This is why I stayed away. This is why we can't be together."

"You didn't do this."

"It's the same."

"No, it's different. Wrong." *I know why he left you now.* Those had been Delana's words and they bothered her. Why had she said them? The order was wrong. I know why *he* left *you.* If James were the abuser wouldn't Delana think it would be the other way round? Wouldn't she have suspected that Michelle left James? And her accusation felt scared and rehearsed. This wasn't the darkness, this was something worse. She covered James's hand and said softly not sure it would work, "You did not do this. You are not going to hurt me. I am safe with you."

He shook his head. "Michelle—"

"Trust me this time. Let me bandage your hand then help me look in her room."

"I won't see anything."

"There's a lot you can notice without sight."

SHE DIDN'T KNOW what she was looking for, but Michelle knew something was off. She saw Delana's bag near the bed.

She lifted it up, surprised by how heavy it was. She zipped it open and saw it stuffed with clothes. "Looks like she was going somewhere."

"She didn't tell me," James said. "I thought she was happy here."

Michelle turned the suitcase upside to empty the contents on the bed. "Why did she come here?"

"I met her when I was recovering at a retreat here on the island. She was sweet and kept my spirits up. It was probably a couple weeks after I'd left that she called me up one day said she needed to get away from trouble at home. I needed a cook so I said she could stay here. I didn't ask too many questions."

Michelle shuffled through Delana's clothes. "You gave her your number?"

"I must have. How else would she call me?"

Good question. "Does your family know about her?"

"Probably."

"I saw a bruise on her face yesterday. She covered it well with makeup." Michelle turned to James when she felt him grow still. "I know it wasn't you because she hinted at another man. She said you saved her. Perhaps her family troubles have followed her."

"I did sense a presence."

"When?"

"But I wasn't sure." He swept his hands over the clothes then stopped when he felt something hard. He moved the clothes aside.

"What is it?" Michelle asked, but the sound of cars and sirens stopped James reply. She rushed to the window and saw the police approaching. How could they have gotten here so fast? The time from Delana arriving at the hospital and police arriving on their doorstep seemed too perfect to be coincidental. Michelle turned and saw James shoving his hands in his pockets. "It's okay, love. I know they're coming for me." He gave her a sad smile. "I guess I won't get my one night after all."

"Yes you will." Michelle quickly stuffed Delana's things back in her bag. She didn't want the police wondering why they'd been looking through her things.

"After you make a statement and they clear you, you are to leave this island," James said resigned.

Michelle put the bag back near the bed and quickly surveyed the room to make sure it looked the same as when they'd entered it. "I'm not leaving."

"I know you're not leaving *yet,* but—"

She heard pounding on the door and left the room.

James followed her, his hand dragging along the wall to keep him oriented. "Michelle, slow down."

The pounding grew louder.

"Michelle, don't do this."

She stopped and turned to him. "I have to." Her heart raced, this was her chance to make things right. James needed her and she wouldn't fail him this time. "I made a mistake before. All those years ago, I shouldn't have let you go."

"You didn't have a choice."

"I do now. I'm not leaving this island without you." She kissed him then raced down the stairs.

CHAPTER 42

Not on her island.

Cathy Lin looked at the grim pictures of Delana's battered face and bruises with studied detachment. Few felt this assault would be resolved, especially considering the attacker. St. Clarine didn't have the attention or resources nor was it as well known as its sister islands. Centuries ago, the island had been like a beautiful woman who had caught the eye of two dangerous yet powerful men—namely the British and the French—who'd descended on her to rape her of her riches until there was little left before they discarded the island to the Dutch, briefly the Portuguese and then the British, again, before they managed to gain independence.

But by then, the infrastructure was damaged by greed and corruption. Only recently, a new patriotism had risen, and the island people used their wiles to set themselves apart and export a unique fruit native only to the island. The market for the fruit was too small for bigger industries to take notice, but big enough to provide the island with much needed revenue.

But enough money was still a problem, so tourism and island

thrill seekers were still their largest moneymaker, but with them came trouble. Especially the wealthy ones. As a little girl she'd been warned about rich foreigners too quick to flash their white teeth and paper money. Her grandfather had been one of the Chinese immigrants brought over to work the railroads and her family had risen in status. Her brother worked in government and a sister was a professor. Her parents had been grossly disappointed that she'd chosen to be a police officer. But Cathy felt it was her calling.

She remembered a friend being taken and never found. They had always parted at the railroad crossing after school, but she had never made it home. It had frightened her and she didn't like to be frightened. The police kept order; they knew things. She would protect her island and its people the best way she knew how. One day she would make commissioner. Right now she had a criminal to convict. Presently she had him sitting in one of their cells. The worst she could find. He hadn't protested, to his credit, but she expected a high priced lawyer to show up shortly. The woman who had arrived with him was adamant that he was innocent. But of course, as his wife, she would say that.

Cathy believed Delana. She was a true island girl who had come from a good family. From what Cathy had understood she'd gone to work for the wealthy Winfield man. She'd pitied him because of his blindness and he'd misinterpreted her tender care for something more. He'd gone into a rage. How Winfield's wife played into the picture she'd uncover later. For now she had to put her case together. Before influence and money came to tear it apart.

Cathy didn't raise her head when her door flew open. She knew who would come in—a man running like he'd disturbed a hornet's nest.

"Did you have to arrest him?" Forton da Silva demanded.

Cathy looked at him. Despite his six foot frame, Forton would jump at the sight of a mosquito. Anything could make him nervous. He liked rules and regulations. He liked keeping his closet full of fine Italian shoes and French designer clothes. He liked his weekly trips to the barber and his house on the hill. Keeping rich people happy had gotten him that.

The only people Cathy cared about were the school children playing in the yard, the people in the market and the hard working islanders coming home after a long day. She would fight for Delana.

"Yes, I did."

Forton closed the door and tugged on his tie. "Do you know who he is?"

"I don't care who he is."

"You should care. You have to tread lightly when it comes to people like him."

"We've tread far too lightly." They had yet to convict one rapist. Most domestic incidents ended with only a fine, and they'd had three disappearances within the past two years that hadn't been solved. All trails led to the wealthy visitors who disappeared when the police got too close. The Winfield man wouldn't be able to if she could help it. Lucky for Delana, she had a wealthy ally who would help them make a solid case.

DELANA WAS LYING, but she had no way to prove it. Michelle sat on the floor of her cell and sighed. Assaulting a police officer. What injustice. She'd accidentally hit him in the face with her elbow when he'd tried to restrain her from giving James a hug. And how convenient that there had been photographers as the police led her and James to the station. Must be a slow news day.

Unfortunately, no one would listen to protestations of James's innocence and no one would tell her how he was doing. She doubted even after her release that she'd be allowed to see him.

And she had no way to talk to Delana and find out what she was hiding. But why would she lie? Just yesterday she'd said James was so sweet. Why had Delana suddenly decided to leave? Did it have anything to do with Michelle's sudden arrival?

At least the police had allowed her to call one person. She'd called Martha and told her that James was being charged with assault and battery. After Martha stopped laughing, Michelle told her she wasn't joking. She said a lawyer was on her way. But Michelle could tell that the Detective Inspector Lin was determined to see James behind bars and it did look bad for him. Michelle hadn't been in the house to witness anything.

How had he hurt his hand? What had he been doing in her room?

Don't touch me! She remembered Delana's frightened gaze when Michelle had come towards her, as if she were afraid Michelle would harm her too. Why would she think that...or did she know something about her? Perhaps she knew about Michelle's gift and was afraid of what Michelle could reveal. But they'd never met so how would she know anything? Unless James had told her...or somebody else.

Joanna perhaps? No, she loved her son too much. She wouldn't want to see him hurt. But why hadn't Martha mentioned her or James?

Michelle rubbed her tired eyes. If she wanted to help James, and prove to him that he hadn't hurt her, she'd have to uncover what Delana was truly afraid of.

CHAPTER 43

Kenneth looked at the online story with the grim interest of a bystander unable to tear their gaze away from a car crash. He couldn't believe what he was seeing.

He quickly closed his laptop when he heard the doorbell. He glanced across the living room at his nanny Joyce playing with his son Alex, who giggled with delight. He heard his daughter Syrah greeting Wendy at the door. She and Jessie were scheduled for tennis. "Hi," Wendy said, bouncing into the room wearing a cute white tennis skirt and blue blouse which matched her eyes.

Kenneth smiled back, trying to appear casual. "Jasmine will be down in a minute."

"Okay." She bent down and petted their golden retriever Dion, who had pressed his wet nose against her olive-toned leg seeking more attention.

He hesitated asking her about what he'd seen, but before he could, her phone alerted her to a message. She glanced down, read for a few seconds then swore.

"St. Clarine?" Kenneth guessed.

Wendy nodded then looked at Joyce and switched to French

knowing neither she nor Syrah understood it. "It couldn't be her, though. Could it?"

"It looks like her."

Wendy took a seat looking worried then made a dismissive wave of her hand. "Fortunately, the incident is too small for it to become international news."

"*We* know about it."

"Only because we're interested." Although neither was from St. Clarine they both liked to keep abreast of various Caribbean news.

"Does Jessie know?"

"Not yet," he said.

Jessie came into the room, swinging her tennis racket. "What are you two talking about?"

Kenneth cleared his throat. "I'm sorry, Joyce, but could you excuse us a minute?"

She nodded and took Alex away.

Wendy looked at Kenneth and continued in French, "Do you want me to tell her?"

"Let her see it first," he replied.

"I don't think she should see the picture until she hears it from someone."

Jessie rested her hands on her hips. "That's very rude, you know. Typical French."

"We're not French," they both said in unison.

Jessie held up her hands in surrender knowing she'd hit a colonial sore spot. "Okay, okay. What are you talking about?"

"Where's Michelle?" Kenneth asked.

Jessie shrugged. "Traveling on business. Why?"

He sighed.

Jessie became concerned. "What's going on?"

"Michelle was arrested in St. Clarine."

"That can't be."

"It's online," Wendy said. "They said she assaulted an officer."

Jessie slowly sat down. "That's impossible. That doesn't sound like Michelle. And why would it make the news?"

Kenneth clasped his hands and leaned forward. "Because the case involves her ex-husband—"

"Estranged," Jessie corrected him

"James Winfield."

"Looks like a case of sex and money," Wendy said. "He beat up his mistress. At least that's what the story said. He'd been living with her on the island."

"A mistress? James?" Jessie shook her head. "No way."

Kenneth showed her the image online. "This is what he allegedly did to her."

They sat in silence then Kenneth said, "Perhaps your concerns about him were right."

"But what was she doing down there with him?" Jessie said. "Why did she say it was a business trip? Do you think she knew he was down there all this time?"

"We won't know until we ask her."

"We'll have to tell Teresa."

"Not yet, let's find out more first."

HE COULDN'T FIND MUCH ELSE about the case. Another news story mentioned that the victim had been James's cook and that he'd allegedly demanded a more intimate relationship. Presently, it looked bad for him.

Jessie entered the living room holding Alex. "Could you hold him a minute while I get his bottle?"

Kenneth didn't look up from the screen of his laptop. "Where's Joyce?"

"I gave her the night off since I cancelled with Wendy."

Kenneth motioned to the ground. "Just put him down and I'll watch him."

"I'm not asking you to *watch* him. I'm asking you to hold him for one sec—"

"Just put him down," Kenneth repeated with less patience.

"Kenneth—"

"I don't want to hurt him."

"You won't."

"You don't know that. I could hold his head wrong or something. He needs to be a little stronger. He's too helpless."

"He's sturdier than he looks. Kenneth, this isn't hard."

Kenneth snapped his laptop closed. "It's hard for me. I told you that. I'm not ready yet."

Jessie looked at him for a long moment. "Sometimes you act as if he were an accident. I thought we both wanted this."

"I thought it would be easier." Kenneth stood, unable to take the hurt in her eyes and headed for the kitchen.

She followed him. "Easier than what?"

He set his laptop on the kitchen table. "Just easier." He opened the fridge and pulled out a bottle of orange juice. "Let's not talk about this right now. I'm trying to think of ways to help your sister—"

"All I asked—"

He slammed the fridge door closed. "Just be patient with me!"

"Patient? I discover my brother-in-law has been arrested for allegedly beating up his mistress, my sister may have been lying to me for years, and my husband won't hold his son for one minute and you think it's because I'm not being patient!"

Kenneth set the bottle on the counter and sighed with regret. "I'm sorry. I know I'm being unfair. I didn't expect to feel this way." He closed his eyes and rubbed his forehead. "Maybe we shouldn't have…" He stopped.

But it was too late. When he looked at his wife's face he knew he'd gone too far. Jessie stared at him wide eyed. "Maybe we shouldn't have what? Go on say it. Maybe we shouldn't have had him." She looked down at Alex and cradled him close. "Maybe we shouldn't have fallen in love. Maybe we shouldn't have gotten married. Maybe there are a lot of things we shouldn't have done. But it's too late to back out now."

Syrah rushed into the kitchen. "What happened? I heard something bang."

"It's nothing," Jessie said. "Could you hold Alex for a minute? Oh, and here's his bottle and blanket. I'll meet you in the nursery in a minute. Thanks."

Kenneth waited for Syrah to leave before he said, "Jasmine, I didn't mean it like that."

She folded her arms. "How did you mean it?"

He shook his head. "I'm sorry. I don't know what I'm saying."

"Yes, you do. Do you want space? I can take—"

He reached for a glass then changed his mind and faced her. "I'm not Sean."

She paused. "I never said—"

"I know you want me to be. I heard you say it." He remembered when his brother-in-law Sean and Jessie's sister Teresa came to visit and Jessie had been setting up Alex's bath in the kitchen sink, a hooded baby towel, and diapers were set out nearby.

"Is it bath time?" Sean said with a big smile, lifting Alex out of his chair, making him giggle. "Can I help?"

"Sure."

He expertly tested the water to make sure it was the right temperature before lowering Alex into the few inches of water. Using a soapy washcloth he began wiping Alex down. "He's a little scrawny," he said, rubbing Alex's tummy. "I like chubby babies. Are you sure you're feeding him enough?" he teased.

"He's got a fast metabolism."

Kenneth watched from a distance. He envied Sean's ease as he frequently used a cup and poured water over Alex to keep him warm.

"You look like you're having more fun than he is," Jessie said.

"Used to be Chloe's favorite time," Sean said referring to his daughter who had passed. A sad look crossed his features then left. "Besides, he's a happy baby."

"He gets that from his father," Jessie said, smiling at Kenneth.

He returned her smile although he didn't mean it. His son had a happy disposition most times but he also had a pair of lungs too. His nose would turn red when he was ready to wail. The first time had shocked him, scared him. He recalled trying to make soothing noises and rubbing his little arms and legs but he couldn't seem to calm him. He'd never tried again.

Kenneth watched Sean dry and wrap Alex up in a towel. His son grinned, looking warm and cozy.

"Now you're all clean," Sean said. "Let's get you dressed."

Jessie slapped her forehead. "His clothes. I knew I was forgetting something."

"I'll get it," Kenneth said, wanting to feel useful. He returned to the kitchen, hoping to impress Jessie with what he'd selected when he overheard her say in a low voice, "Sean's amazing with kids.

Teresa laughed. "If it were up to him, he'd have five of his own."

"And you?"

There was a smile in her voice when she spoke. "We'll come up with a compromise."

"You're lucky."

Teresa shook her head. "Don't compare. Sean grew up in a tight loving family, Kenneth didn't."

He couldn't remember what Jessie had said in return. He only remembered her words and the longing in her voice *You're lucky.* He knew she meant: You're lucky to have a man like him. You're lucky to have a husband like him. Your child will be lucky to have a father like him. Not like the one I have. And it hurt because he didn't know how to change.

"I don't know what you heard," Jessie said, "but I never meant—" She leaned against the counter and folded her arms. "How long am I supposed to pretend that we're okay? Pretend that we're happy new parents? You know you're better at pretending than I am."

"I'm not pretending. I am happy."

She slowly nodded. "That's good because I'm not." She pushed herself from the counter. "But you're right. Let's not talk about this right now. My sister is in trouble and we have to help her. After that..." She shrugged then turned and left the kitchen leaving the statement open and hanging in the air like an ominous coming storm.

CHAPTER 44

Jessie didn't join Syrah in the nursery right away. She sat on the steps and took a deep breath to calm her temper. She couldn't let Syrah suspect that anything was seriously wrong.

She pressed her fist to her eyes. Lies. Lies. Lies. Her life felt like a series of lies. Michelle lying about James. Michelle lying about her business trip. And she had her own lies too. She was lying about how happy she and Kenneth were with Alex. It was all a lie. Everyone congratulating them when in truth Kenneth was too afraid to hold his own son. She knew the reason but it didn't make it hurt less.

She knew it was unfair to take her frustration out on him. But she was tired and edgy. She didn't want to feel like a single parent in a two parent household. The nanny gave her all the support she needed, but she wanted Kenneth to take up his role. She wanted to see him pick up and hold his son. Interact with him, even briefly. She didn't need him to be doting, but he avoided him every chance he got. Perhaps she was asking too much. Perhaps when Alex was a year or two it would be different.

But that was her true fear—that it wouldn't change. That Kenneth would show a preference to Syrah that Alex would eventually see and never understand. He was a good man and she wanted to give him time. But how much would he need? How much could she give?

Jessie rose to her feet. She would figure that out later. Right now she had to come up with the right story to tell Teresa so they could help Michelle.

Teresa sighed. "Bertha predicted this," Teresa said the following day as she, Sean, Jessie and Kenneth sat in the Preston living room.

Jessie's eyebrows shot up. "What? That our brother-in-law is a possible abuser?"

"James is not an abuser."

"You said Michelle had to worry about a monster and you thought it was James."

"I thought it *might* be him," Teresa said. "But I wasn't certain. After talking to Bertha I now know it isn't. If he had a dark side she would have sensed it."

"What do you think is going on then?"

"I don't know."

Kenneth spoke up. "I'll schedule a flight to go down there and—"

"You can't do that," Sean said.

"Why not?"

Sean turned to his wife. "Tell them what Bertha said."

Teresa rubbed her hands together. "She told me that Michelle would go on a trip and that I was to let her go until she came back and asked for our help."

"But she needs our help *now*," Jessie said.

"No, Michelle will find her way out of this. She usually does. Bertha told me that Michelle and James have to heal the wounds of the past. It's not our place to interfere."

Jessie threw up her hands. "But they're in jail!"

"They won't stay there," Sean said. "From what I understand he's got strong family connections."

"But what about Michelle? Assault on a police officer is a serious offense."

"I don't think James would leave her there," Kenneth said. "She's his wife."

"Wouldn't be the first time a husband let his wife down," Jessie said under her breath.

Kenneth looked away.

Teresa and Sean looked at the pair sensing the tension between them. Sean sent Teresa a questioning look; she shrugged.

"I'm with Kenneth," Sean said. "Even with a mistress, I don't see Winfield letting his wife get caught up in his mess."

"We can hope," Jessie said. "But the truth is we don't know anything about him anymore. And I'm not sure I know Michelle either."

"Michelle is going to come to us for help one day," Teresa said. "And that day will come soon."

Jessie rubbed her forehead. "Michelle likes doing things on her own, taking charge. She never asks anyone for help."

"One day she's going to have to."

"I HATE the thought of just waiting," Jessie said as she changed for bed. Kenneth sat staring at the marble chess set he'd placed on a side table in the corner. "I know it's the best thing to do, but it doesn't make it any easier."

He moved a piece.

Jessie climbed into bed. "I still can't wrap my mind around Michelle going to see him."

Kenneth continued to stare at the board.

"Do you think she was secretly seeing him all this time?"

Kenneth moved another chess piece.

Jessie sighed. He'd been quiet since Teresa and Sean left. He had a right to be angry. She was angry with him too. Perhaps they really needed space. Time away. He needed time and patience and she wasn't giving it to him. Another wife would, knowing what he'd suffered. "When Michelle comes back, I think I'll take Alex and stay at the family house for a while. That way—"

Kenneth swept the chess pieces to the ground in one angry motion. "Don't do that. I hate it."

Jessie looked down at the scattered pieces, startled then lifted her gaze to his face. "What?"

"Don't threaten to leave me. You know how much that hurts." He rested his arms on the table and hung his head in misery. "I'm sorry you're unhappy. I'm sorry I've disappointed you as a husband, as a father—"

"No, you haven't," Jessie said, alarmed by the pain in his voice. She jumped out of bed and rushed over, eager to comfort him. On her way, she stepped on a chess piece, the sharp edge pinching into the sole of her foot. She silently swore and hopped the rest of the way, glad he was looking down so he didn't see her. She gathered him in her arms, resting his head against her chest. "I'm not unhappy with you or the marriage. I just—"

Kenneth drew away from her and stood. "Want me to be a better man."

Jessie violently shook her head. "No, you're..." She didn't

want to say 'perfect' because they both knew he wasn't. She watched him bend down and pick up the chess pieces. She knelt down and helped him. "You mean everything to me. It's...sometimes I'm not sure I'm the right one. I have a temper. I'm not always patient. I'm not always understanding and I thought time away would give us a chance to deal with our fears. It wouldn't be permanent it would—" She stopped when she realized he wasn't listening. He put the pieces on the board then looked out the window at the dark sky. She'd hurt him and hadn't realized how much. She walked over to him and set the pieces she'd gathered down. "I'm sorry. I won't leave you. I'll never mention it again."

He didn't look at her, when he spoke his voice was soft. "Whatever the problem we'll solve it. Together."

She nodded. "Yes."

"You, Syrah and Alex..." He bit his lip and shook his head. "You don't know how much you mean to me. I'll try harder to make you happy—"

Jessie made a sound of frustration and grabbed his chin, forcing him to look at her. "I've said this before and I'll say it again. Your job isn't to make me happy. Right now I'm still adjusting to the role of being the mother to an infant. My husband's afraid to hold his son, I understand, but it's still frustrating. My sister Teresa is talking about monsters coming and my other sister is in jail possibly married to a man who beat up his mistress."

His gaze grew tender. "Jasmine—"

She rested her hands on her hips. "I don't like not knowing what to do. I have a temper and I'm not always the best at controlling it." She took a deep breath and held his gaze. "Your job, Mr. Preston, is to love me anyway. Think you can do that?"

Kenneth drew her into his arms. Jessie felt the tension

between them disappear and tears of relief filled her eyes. He held her in a warm embrace and whispered, "I always will."

CHAPTER 45

They wanted to settle. James had been denied bail. He still sat in a cold cell and they wanted to settle. The thought made Michelle's stomach turn. But Michelle hadn't had much hope when she'd met with James's lawyer in a downtown hotel after being released. Georgia Kent reminded Michelle of a wilted banana. Brown-skinned, petite, dressed in a sharp suit and shabby heels, she had the depressed face of a woman who always expected rain. Michelle had imagined the Winfields hiring a lawyer who was savvier; had more determination but Georgia looked ready to wave a flag of surrender. They sat in a private booth in the hotel restaurant. "It doesn't look good," she said with a sigh. She squeezed lemon into her glass of water. "It's her word against his and she's very sympathetic. The fact that he's blind could help a little, but not much. He's a big man and strong. The fact that he's wealthy doesn't help either."

"That's why they're paying you."

Georgia shot her a look before lifting her water. She took a sip. "I am being paid to assess and handle the situation and do what's best for my client."

And for yourself, Michelle thought. The lawyer didn't look as if she wanted to fight hard. "The Winfield's think he's guilty, don't they? And you do too."

"He doesn't remember anything and he can't explain his bruises."

She was dancing around the answer, but Michelle knew it was 'yes'. The Winfield's had given up on him. *Since I was nine*, James had said, *I knew I was cursed*. They all thought this was the reason. The beast had returned. But Michelle sensed that wasn't true. "He's innocent."

"You're his wife, right?"

"That's not the point."

"Of course it's the point. You have to believe in him. I completely understand. Your reputation is on the line."

"No one is considering that Delana may be lying."

Georgia took another sip of her water then set it down. "Her injuries are real and that's the only thing anyone is going to focus on." She waved a finger before Michelle could speak. "Even if I managed to get a non-jury trial, I don't think I can convince a judge of that. James has two options. Agree to a lesser charge or settle."

"Either way he admits to being guilty."

Georgia bristled at her tone. "I don't know why I'm sharing all this with you anyway."

Michelle smiled. "Because I asked you to." *And I convinced you that you wanted to.* Persuading her to speak hadn't been as hard as she'd imagined. Martha had given her the lawyer's contact information; meeting with her at the hotel then persuading her to share her strategy hadn't been difficult.

"The Winfields want to quietly settle this. I would suggest you convince him that it's his best option. He won't have to admit to anything. With a decent cheque amount dangling in front of them, mainly her, I don't think it will take much effort to make this all go away."

SHE WOULDN'T HAVE James branded a criminal. More so, she didn't want *him* to think he was. Settling meant he was admitting to being culpable somehow and Michelle knew he wasn't. She just had to find a way to prove it.

That afternoon Michelle went to the hospital, snuck past the busy nurse's station, walked down a long corridor and into Delana's room. Fortunately, only two other beds were occupied— one with a woman snoring, her red wig sitting on the stand beside her, another with a woman listening to something flowing through her large headphones.

Michelle walked over to Delana's bed, which was near the window on the far wall, and held up her hands when Delana's eyes widen with fear. "I won't touch you. I'm only here to talk."

Delana sat up and gathered her bed sheets closer. "I have nothing to say."

Michelle sat down beside her bed. "I wanted to apologize for not believing you."

Delana let her grip ease a little. "It's okay."

"It's only...when I was returning to the house, I thought I saw a man running out back."

"You saw him?"

Michelle narrowed her eyes. "Clearly you saw him too."

"No. I mean—" Delana shook her head. "You're trying to trick me."

Michelle motioned to Delana's facial scars. "We both know James didn't do this. He helped you. He was kind to you. Why would you want to see him go to jail?"

"He won't go to jail."

"He's in jail now."

"But he won't stay there. Not for long. He's rich. He'll settle this and then it will be over."

Michelle nodded. "Is that what he told you?"

"Who?"

"The man you're protecting."

Delana turned to the window. "I'm not protecting anyone."

"You're scared. You've been acting strange since yesterday morning. What happened?"

"I can't say anything to you. He could hurt my family." She looked at Michelle. "He has money like James and power. I can't make him angry. Please. He told me it won't be a lot of money to settle everything and then we can be together."

"But—"

She returned her gaze to the window. "You should leave. He could hurt you too."

"Okay, I'll leave." Michelle lightly patted Delana's hand as if in farewell. "I'll let you rest. You look tired." She let her voice slow. "Very, very tired."

Delana yawned. "I am tired."

"Exhausted."

Delana's eyes grew heavy. "Yes." She yawned again and rested down. "Thanks for understanding and letting me sleep." She closed her eyes.

Michelle rested her hand on top of Delana's, and with her free hand turned on a recorder before she said in a soft voice, "You need to rest in order to be strong. Lying takes so much effort. I know you want to protect him because you love him. But you want to protect us even more because you know what he can do. You want to tell me everything and you don't have to be scared because I know it all."

Delana frowned but kept her eyes closed. "You know about the sleeping pills? How I would sometimes put them in James's food and drink..."

Michelle took a deep breath determined to keep her voice steady, in spite of her shock. "Yes, I knew."

"He told me I was helping James and I wanted to. James didn't always sleep well even at the retreat. Sometimes he'd looked so tired. I thought a good night's sleep would help. It was harmless. But then..." She shook her head.

"But then what?"

"But then he wanted me to poison you. And I almost did. I put rat poison in the eggs, but I couldn't go through with it. He was so angry."

"And he's scary when he's angry."

Delana bit her lip. "Yes. But he isn't always angry. When he isn't he's wonderful."

"What happened the other day? Who hit you?"

"We're so happy together."

"What's the name of the man who hit you?"

"He said he'd visit me. When will he visit me?"

"Delana what's his name?"

"And we'll leave here together. I did everything he told me to. He won't be angry now."

Michelle sighed. She'd lost her connection with Delana. She'd been able to channel her fear to persuade her to speak, but her fear and affection for this unknown man was stronger and Michelle couldn't seem to break it because she didn't know enough about Delana to manipulate her thoughts. But at least she'd gotten Delana to confess to giving James sleeping pills and trying to poison her. That would ruin any settlement. But didn't prove James's innocence. The prosecution could argue that James had found out what she had done and that was why he'd attacked her.

Michelle left the room then stopped when she saw a familiar figure talking to one of the nurses. She jumped back inside the room, drew open a curtain and hid behind it. She saw the shadow of the man as he passed her.

A man from the past.

A man James had once trusted.

CHAPTER 46

She was right behind him.

Graham softly swore when he saw Michelle's face reflected behind him in the window of his silver Porsche. Graham made sure his sunglasses were firmly in place before he turned around and said, "What a surprise."

Michelle folded her arms as they both stood outside his car. "Cut the crap. You—"

He held up his hand. "Before you begin, let me get one thing clear. I don't get caught. You may figure this all out and I may tell you some things. But by the time you tell anyone what you think I did or didn't do I'll be long gone."

"You tried to kill us."

Graham shook his head. "No, only you." His voice turned cold. "You ruined a perfect life. *My* life. You were the beginning of the end for me and I didn't even see it. The first moment James saw you I should have seen what was coming. But I under-estimated you. We all did. I hate being wrong." He raised his voice. "Are you recording this? Yes, that's right, I wanted you dead."

"You planned to kill me and have James charged with murder?"

His voice returned to normal. "No, you'd just disappear. You might not have heard, but another unfortunate woman disappeared here years ago. Never solved. You'd suffer the same fate. Your body would never be found. If Delana hadn't panicked it would have worked. I had to come up with a new strategy to get rid of you."

"Assault and battery."

He shrugged. "I knew why James left you all those years ago, remember? I thought the past should repeat itself."

"Why? James trusted you."

"I did it for the money. I'm not a fool. James stopped trusting me the moment he met you. And after you and James ran off, Joanna didn't trust me much either. I managed to hang around long enough because Joanna was a mess when James left. However, when James finally returned with Joanna, as we knew he would, things were never the same. Don't know why he felt the need to go back to London. It was only six months, maybe nine, before the shit really hit the fan. The home invasion," Graham said with a cynical smile. "Left James in a coma and put my future on shaky ground. I had to think fast. I travelled with James here to St. Clarine, but I still needed insurance and I found an insurer."

"Who?"

He glanced at the sky. "I feel like a drink." He looked at her. "My treat."

"I'd never go anywhere with you. Who did you go to?"

"You still don't realize how valuable James is to the Winfields. Even after his attack, his mind was as sharp as ever. They depend on him and his keen insights."

"Who?"

He flashed a cruel smile. "I'm not sure I want to tell you."

Michelle reached out to touch him.

He blocked her hand and his smile fell. "No, don't try your witchcraft on me. I know all about you. Are you still recording this?"

"I'm not recording anything. And I don't care about a parasite like you. Who are you working for?"

He shook his head and clicked his tongue in pity. "Still haven't guessed? To me it was obvious."

"Stop playing games."

He lifted up his sunglasses revealing a bruised eye. "Is this what you were trying to see?" He pulled the sunglasses back in place. "Hurt like a bitch, but I had to trick James into hitting something." Graham had gone into James's room and whispered words to provoke him to respond while he was still asleep.

Michelle turned. "You're wasting my time."

Graham leaned against his car and said, "James really was a wreck when he left you. I think the attack in his apartment did him some good. He was in pain anyway. It gave him something to focus on."

Michelle spun around. "Were you behind the home invasion?"

He placed a hand on his chest in mock horror. "The thought. Why would I do such a thing? I've known him since he was a kid."

"That's why he trusted you."

"That was his fault. You don't trick me and think you can get away with it. It's not my fault he still thought I worked for him. When he came to this island I helped him find the property he purchased. I knew the location was perfect to keep him isolated and away from everything. I would suggest you do the same. There are a lot more skeletons in the Winfield closet."

"Where's Joanna?"

"Haven't you guessed who I work for yet?" Graham folded his arms and rocked on his heels. "No? Let's just say his Aunt Angela isn't the doting aunt she likes to pretend to be. She's still nervous about Cory's place in the family. If something were to happen to James..." He let his words trail off and shrugged. "Cory has no idea what his dear mother would do for him."

"Where's Joanna?"

Graham opened his car door. "Do you know why I told you all this? Because you still have no idea what and who you're dealing with." He laughed. "No idea at all." He sat in the driver's seat and looked up at her. "It was nice knowing you. We might meet again, but I doubt it."

CHAPTER 47

Michelle held James's hand as they sat in a private jet soaring high over the Caribbean Sea. She couldn't wait to get home. James was free. Georgia had been able to present Delana with the evidence that she'd lied and after hearing her voice on the recording she admitted the truth. Graham had hit her and after she'd regained consciousness, he'd told her what she was supposed to do and say. Graham, as predicted, was nowhere to be found. But Michelle didn't care, James was safe and vindicated. Now she only had to convince him that their nightmare was over.

He'd tentatively said yes to returning to the States with her, to spending some time at her house, but he hadn't said he'd stay.

"All that's happened still doesn't mean we can be together," he'd told her on the drive back to his place in St. Clarine after he'd been released from jail.

Michelle stared at him surprised by his words. "Of course it does. It proves the curse is broken. Graham hurt Delana. He may have been involved in your home invasion attack too."

James didn't react with much surprise to Graham's treachery

and when she asked about his mother he pulled something from his trouser pocket and held it up instead. "They thought this was mine."

Michelle glanced at the item and saw it was a man's diamond pinkie ring. "That's Graham's ring."

He nodded. "I felt it when we were searching through Delana's things."

"So you knew?"

"I suspected. I guessed by the shape and the feel…and the energy."

"But you didn't say anything."

"If things went really bad I would have."

"You should have told me. You should have spoken up sooner. It would have helped solve everything."

James slipped the ring back in his pocket. His voice was quiet. "Not everything. He wasn't there that night."

His words sobered her. That night. She still remembered that awful night, the claw marks on her back, the blood on his fingers, the dark energy in the house. But she still felt they had a second chance. She'd proven that when she put her mind to something she could succeed. She was returning home victorious. Her business was safe and James was free. Anything was possible.

She looked at him now. He sat with his head back and his eyes closed. She lightly touched his arm. "Are you alright?"

"I'm fine."

"What are you thinking about?"

James started to smile. "That you still owe me one night."

CHAPTER 48

He wanted a thousand nights with her. More. A hush, still evening surrounded Michelle's darkened bedroom. James groaned low in his throat as he sank deeper into the pure pleasure he found between his wife's thighs, inhaling the sweet scent of her skin. His hands explored the curves of her body—her back, her waist, her hips, her thighs—and remembered every soft line. His body burned with heat but she was chocolate ginger ice cream—rich, creamy and cool to the touch. It was just what he needed to keep from setting them both aflame. She knew how to touch him, where to touch him, what he needed.

But the pleasure brought pain. She wanted to deny what he was, but he'd never put her at risk again. He knew what he was truly capable of. He knew the darkness still followed him.

He could only have one more night, that was the only reprieve his body would allow. Tonight he would make love to her with every fiber of his being. He would cherish her, worship her, adore her as he had the moment he knew she was his. With each taste of her lips, touch of her hand he felt himself slipping away, drawn to the dark abyss he'd once thought he'd conquered.

He could no longer fight it. Instead he would surrender. He would give all of himself to her and hold nothing back. No matter what it cost him.

I love you so much, she said.

But he was too far gone to reply with words so he wrapped her in a memory of love that spanned all time.

And Michelle held onto him, her bare body wrapped so tight around his as if they were one, so she wouldn't be swept away by the swirling visions of different places, different races, different ages, different times. But what remained constant was the depth of unwavering love. His love. She felt it all around them and felt buoyant.

She'd won. She'd beaten the darkness. Her love meant something. She saw their future together. A bright future where he wouldn't be isolated by his limitations. He could be part of the world again. She imagined describing what the CCBE looked like now, giving him a tour and introducing him to the people she worked with. She imagined having her sisters and their families over for dinner and reuniting him with them. She imagined their home together, going on holidays and the life they would share.

But what she didn't imagine was waking up the next morning and James not doing the same.

CHAPTER 49

At first she thought he was pretending as she tried to rouse him to wake, but when he didn't move a feeling of dread crept over her. "James?" She shook him.

She shook him harder.

He didn't move.

She felt his arms, his neck, held his face in her hands. "James can you hear me? James!" Her voice became frantic. "James, honey, please...please I can't lose you again. Don't leave me like this." Her mind began to spin. Was this why he made no promises to stay, why last night had felt like a final goodbye? Had she truly failed him in the end? Was the power of her love a lie?

Michelle gripped her hands into fists, stealing herself against emotions that threatened to destroy her. No, she would not think about that right now. She wouldn't panic, she wouldn't despair. She had to stay in control and think. He was still warm to the touch and had a pulse, he was alive.

She dialed the emergency number and gave them his medical history.

But he didn't respond in the ambulance and hours later

doctors remained baffled as to what was wrong with him. She told them everything she knew about his past illnesses, but nothing worked. Michelle sat alone in the waiting room as they conducted more tests. The doctors seemed to be giving up hope. They spoke to her about keeping him comfortable or considering life ending options, which she flatly refused. He was still in there. She knew it. She would fight for him. If he still breathed, there was still a chance to save him.

But she couldn't save him alone. She took out her cell phone and for the first time, with shaking hands, reached out for help.

"WAKE UP, SWEETS. SOMETHING'S WRONG."

Teresa rubbed her eyes and stared at Sean as he quickly changed. She glanced at the clock. It was two in the morning. It had been a long day and she'd only just managed to drift off to sleep. But by his efficient movements and the look on his face she knew they faced an emergency.

She jumped out of bed now wide awake. "What happened?"

"I just got off the phone with Jessie. Michelle's at the hospital—"

Teresa stared at him alarmed. "How bad are her injuries? Do we—"

Sean shook his head. "She's okay. It's not her. It's James."

Teresa pulled on her shirt then froze as a vision came to her.

He stared at her. "What is it?"

"I just had a terrible feeling."

"Get changed. Your sister will be okay."

Teresa shook her head. "No she won't."

"Why not?"

"Because the monster is here."

On the drive to the hospital Teresa called Bertha, surprised by her friend's tone as if she'd expected her phone call. "I'm sorry to call so early, but it's an emergency. Michelle's asked for help and I sensed the monster again," she said. "What does it mean? What should I do?"

"Call BJ and have him meet you at the hospital."

Teresa thought it was odd that her cousin would need to be present, but trusted her friend's words. "And then what?"

"Remind Michelle to remember the story."

As a doctor, Sean had grown used to delivering bad news. But nothing had prepared him for this moment. He returned to the private waiting room where Teresa, BJ, Jessie, Kenneth and Michelle sat in plush cream chairs that matched the surrounding walls. All eyes turned to him when he entered. He took a deep breath; there was no other way to say it. "He's dying. There's no identifiable reason why, but he is. However, there is brain activity. Two nurses have heard him mumble 'I can't protect her. I have to protect her,' but that's all he'll say. He won't respond to any other stimuli. He's tormented somehow. He's a healthy man, there's no reason he should be in this state. He's willing himself to die." Sean turned to Michelle. "You have to talk to him. Reach him, even if you don't think he's listening."

Michelle shook her head and looked at the ground. "No."

Sean blinked. "I'm sorry?"

"His wife would kill him," Michelle said in a low voice.

"What?"

She lifted her gaze to his. "That's what the prophesy said."

She looked at her sisters. "It said that his wife would kill him. This is what they meant."

Jessie shook her head in frustration. "Mich, you're not making any sense."

"What prophesy?" Teresa asked.

"Did James have a mistress? Were you secretly seeing him all this time?"

"No," Michelle said.

Teresa rolled her eyes. "This is not the time for that."

"I was curious," Jessie said. "Weren't you?"

"James didn't do anything wrong," Michelle said.

"What prophesy?" Teresa repeated.

"I didn't tell you about it because I didn't want to believe it. I thought I was strong enough for anything. He's dying because of me. He's...he's scared he'll hurt me."

"So he did hurt you," Jessie said in a tight, angry voice.

"No, there was something in the house. Something that came over him and it only happened once—"

"Once is enough," Kenneth said in a grim tone.

"It wasn't him! He's not a beast. It was the darkness I sensed all those years ago. Somehow it comes over him. It clings to him, but it's not *him*."

"Remember the story," Teresa said.

Michelle looked at her and frowned. "What?"

"That's what Bertha wanted me to tell you. It's the only way to defeat the monster."

Michelle's lips thinned. She hugged herself and shook her head. "James is not a monster."

"I didn't say he was, I only—"

"You don't understand. This is all my fault. I should have stayed away. This is happening because of me. He's dying because of me."

"I don't believe that," Sean said. "I think he's longing for you. When I was ill, all I could think about was Teresa."

Michelle flashed a bland smile. "That's because Teresa is a healer. I'm not."

"But it's worth a try," Teresa said in a gentle tone.

Michelle's voice turned bitter. "I did try. It didn't work. It will never work." She looked at Kenneth and Jessie then Sean and Teresa. "I envy you. I envy your pure love. James and I don't have that. Never have. It's always been cursed. I was arrogant enough to think I could beat it but I was wrong and he's suffered for it. I won't see him suffer anymore."

"I'm glad to hear it," Martha said, entering the room with Hildie close behind. She looked at the other startled faces and added, "Everything she's said is correct."

Michelle looked at Martha. "When will Joanna get here?"

Martha took a seat. "Joanna won't be coming."

"Why not?"

"Because she's dead."

"Dead?"

"Who's Joanna?" Sean asked Teresa under his breath.

"James's mother," she replied then nudged him to be quiet.

"How could she be dead?" Michelle asked. "When did it happen?"

"These past several years, after he left you, James has been out of control. Joanna thought she could manage him. She was wrong."

Michelle stared at her for a long moment. "You don't think?"

"We don't know. Neither does James. 'She tried to stop me' that's what James told me afterwards. 'That's all I remember.' He wanted to return to you. No one saw what happened. But there were scratches all over her body. It was the same night he was attacked. I thought that maybe you could heal him."

"That's why you sent that lawyer to the island to settle. You believed he had hurt Delana too."

"My grandson is capable of many things. I think it's time we both realize that he's dangerous and let him go."

Sean shook his head. "From what I've seen of his medical history, which is far from complete, I'd say he's more of a danger to himself than anyone else. He's had a series of hospital visits and from the little I can assess his recoveries would have been long and painful."

"He moved a lot so he could get the best care," Michelle said. "He told me he was accident prone."

Sean's gaze sharpened. "Lots of broken bones?"

"Yes."

"Fractures?"

"Yes."

"Unexplained illnesses?"

"Sometimes."

Sean ran a hand through his hair and swore. "I've never seen it taken to this extreme but it's possible."

"What?"

"There was this case when I was practicing in New York of this woman who would take her daughter to different hospitals with various complaints. Nobody made the connection until she went to Illinois and did the same thing. It's called Munchausen by proxy. It's a mental health issue where a caregiver, seeking attention, makes up or causes illness or harm to a person under their care. Some cases are more extreme than others."

"But... Joanna *adored* James," Michelle said unable to believe him. "She was very attentive to him. They truly were accidents. James told me he was playing in the driveway when he was run over by a car at three. Due to his leg braces, he tripped down the stairs when he was six and broke an arm; he had another car accident at nine…" Michelle let her words drift off. "She couldn't have done all that. She sounds like a monster."

"No, *she* wasn't the monster," Teresa said. "The monster's still here." Teresa shifted her gaze to Martha.

Martha sniffed and shook her head. "I didn't do anything wrong."

"The fact that you believe that is what is truly terrifying," Michelle said. "Your daughter was mentally ill, but you decided to protect her."

"I loved my daughter."

"It was greed that drove you. Greed and power. With James dependent he would never strike out on his own. He and his brilliance would stay under the Winfield control."

"That's not true."

"With your wealth and money you shielded your daughter from any suspicion. You made sure her husband stayed gone. You watched from a distance as she took James to hospitals around the globe so no one could make the connection."

"The first time…I really did think it was an accident. She was behind the wheel and didn't know the nanny had let little James play in the drive. I didn't realize she paid the gardener to make up his story until later."

"How did Graham fit into the picture?"

"He was useful. As one of the first responders on the scene, he was suspicious about James's accident. Fortunately, he liked money enough to keep his suspicions to himself. Joanna thought that would be useful since he knew what law enforcement looked for when a child was hospitalized. He also made sure Joanna didn't go too far. James always got the best care. And I knew when he was old enough he could be free. I thought…when he met you…it would all end."

Remember the story. Bertha's words suddenly came to

Michelle's mind. What story and why? Michelle looked at Martha's regal features and thought back to the English cottage and the garden. How Martha seemed to be testing her and how annoyed she'd felt. But now she knew that moment had offered her a clue. Her father, with all his wealth of international tales, never told her the story of the man born cursed as a beast. She remembered her father constantly feeding them with fairytales. And one of his favorites, to her annoyance, had been *The Princess and the Pea*. "You're not listening," he'd constantly chide her.

"It's a silly story about a girl with an obvious skin problem."

He shook his head in disappointment. "Intellectuals always miss the point. Listen with your heart not your head," he'd said. She had heard him but she'd never listened. Now she knew what he and the story had been telling her. *I've been following the wrong story.* Their tale was not a story about a beast or a curse, but something else. Something small. Something like *The Princess and the Pea.* James's true nature, like the princess in the story, could be revealed by something so small no one else would notice it.

"You lied to him," Michelle finally said, her mind becoming clear. "There's no such thing as the curse of the beast. I knew there was a reason I'd never heard that story. You made it up as a way to control him."

Martha kept her head raised, unapologetic. "I didn't have a choice. James tells people that he was around nine when he learned about the curse, but it was sooner than that. It was the day he told he thought his mother had pushed him down the stairs. I got angry and said only wicked children with the heart of the beast made up such things. I said it wasn't real, I told him to be afraid of such imaginings.

"He was about six and trembled with fear then passed out in

my arms. Since that day he blackouts whenever he fights not to remember something awful."

"But you knew he wasn't lying," Michelle said.

"The blackouts protected him. It's important that a child loves its mother. It's the order of things. Joanna truly loved him. You should have seen her with him when he was a baby. She was so happy. I wasn't going to let anyone steal him away from her."

"But it was still all a lie. You lied to a child."

Martha shrugged. "The prophesy was real."

"Yes. His love for me is killing him because all his life he's lived the lies and secrets you and his mother have fed him. How did you do it?"

Martha shook her head.

"You used his special talent," Michelle guessed. "His ability to connect with things from the past. And he's extra vulnerable to it when he's...let's just say at the height of passion?"

Martha smiled, amused. "You don't know what you're talking about."

"You put something in James's flat that influenced his energy. Possibly a silver pin or a decorative ornament, but it bound him to the memory of a dark, possessive love and that's what started to take over him. That's what was in his London flat and came to our house. I thought it was something that Joanna had given us but it wasn't only her I should have been careful of. It was you too."

"There are a people who came bursting forth from flames," Teresa said remembering one of their father's stories. "They are hot, wild and burning with rage. They rage against injustice. They rage against loss. They feed on vengeance."

Hildie spoke up. "That is not who she is. Her heart is dark for another reason."

Martha held up her hand. "Quiet, Hildie." She fixed

Michelle with a look. "I did everything in my power to try to make James happy the best I could. You wouldn't have been able to marry him if it wasn't for me. I tried to free him."

Hildie rested a hand on her shoulder. "It is time I confess something to you."

Martha shook her head. "Now is not the time."

"Yes, it's time I tell them the truth about you and you learn the truth about me."

"No, Hil—"

"I don't believe in happy endings," Hildie said. She looked around the room. "You're all so young. You don't know the pain of regret and bitterness. We've lived with it. We've seen it. Her family has suffered. They had a right to rage. Her father, who had a gift like James's, had his first wife and child stolen from him. He taught her how important it was to keep those you love close to you no matter the price. He never found his wife, child or the people who took them. It haunted him and that kind of anger does not subside. It taints a bloodline."

"No," Teresa said. "A bloodline isn't tainted, only the mind is. It's what you choose to believe and if it's filled with lies—"

"You really believe that?" Kenneth said curious. "That a bloodline isn't tainted?"

"Of course. Look at you. You're nothing like your father or brother."

Jessie took his hand and softly said, "And you never will be."

Hildie's lip curled. "You don't know anything if you believe that."

"I said be quiet," Martha said.

"Despite everything, Martha tried to be different," Hildie continued. "And when I saw you and James I foolishly thought so too. I too, believed in a happy ending. James invited me to his flat and told me about the person he was planning to see to help him get rid of the curse. Martha had been called away on business and he was eager to talk to someone.

"Joanna didn't know I was there when she burst into the place. I hid in the bathroom as she pleaded with James to stay with her a little longer. But he refused to listen. He told her he loved her, but that his life was with you now. Then he turned his back on her. He didn't see her fly into a rage and lift the statue.

"She struck him hard. Once then twice. He lay motionless on the ground so I thought she would stop. But this time she had a look on her face and that look told me she wasn't going to ever let James go. I thought it was time someone did what you should have done years ago. Protect him. I ran out like a wildcat and scratched her. We fought and...she fell back and cracked her head on the table. She was dead. I suppose Graham had been waiting in the car, because he arrived soon after. He helped me arrange things and set up the home invasion story. I didn't want you to know that I'd accidentally killed Joanna. I didn't want to lose our friendship."

Martha patted her hand. "I understand. I forgive you."

Michelle stared at the two women flabbergasted. "But you blamed James for his mother's death," Michelle said. "You convinced him of it."

"At least he was alive." Martha said, resigned to what her friend had just revealed.

"I couldn't risk him making the connection to me also being there that day. He remembered part of his argument with his mother, in time he could remember more. I couldn't risk it," Hildie said, her voice filled with regret.

"In a way it was his fault," Martha said in a sad voice. "Joanna was perfectly normal until she became a mother."

CHAPTER 51

BJ motioned Jessie over to the side. "I don't know if this will help, but remember when I had you read that emerald for me a couple of weeks ago?"

"It was a very sad reading. A painful love if I remember correctly. Why?"

"The stone belonged to Michelle."

"What?"

"Somehow she damaged the stone and wanted me to fix it. She said she threw it but I sensed there was something more." He shrugged. "I'm not sure this helps, but—"

Jessie suddenly looked pensive. "I said there was a block to their love, didn't I?"

"I think so."

She squeezed his arm with affection. "Thanks for telling me. I think I know what we can do." She walked over to Michelle. "You have to go to James as Sean said, but first you have to take off your ring."

"What?"

"The ring is what is blocking you two. It's holding too much energy from the past. The love is too painful, that's what James is responding to." She held out her hand. "Give it to me and go to him."

"Nothing will work," Martha said. "It's too late now. Let him go in peace."

"Don't listen to her," Teresa said. "Take it off."

Michelle covered her hand. "But Dad said this ring gives me power—"

"It was broken for a reason," BJ said. "Its usefulness is gone. It led love to you but now it's keeping it from you. It kept some of the dark energy of the past."

Michelle hesitated. She felt vulnerable without it. What if it didn't work? What if all hope was already lost? "Love alone doesn't work. I need—"

Kenneth knelt in front of her, his gentle gaze holding hers. "Remember what I told you in the coffee shop? You're not alone. Why would you depend on a stone, when you have the power of our love surrounding you?"

Tears blinded her. For the first time she realized what she'd kept from herself—from James. If she'd reached out sooner, spoken to her parents, her sisters, she and James may not have suffered as much as they had. It was her arrogance that had prolonged their parting. But now as she looked at the faces of all those who loved her she realized she didn't have to fight alone, there was no weakness in asking for help, admitting her vulnerabilities.

Michelle slid the ring off her finger and handed it to him, ready to fight once again knowing she had the power of an army behind her.

MICHELLE WENT to James's bedside. As still as he lay, he reminded her of a mountain—awe inspiring, like a mighty volcano. She wouldn't tell him all that she knew yet, just enough to break him free of his torment. She touched his hand. *You're not a beast.* She silently told him. *You are strong, a protector, a husband, a friend. You want to stay with me. You want to live with me.* She saw his brows furrow and knew she'd reached him. She held his hand in both of hers. *You want to stay with me forever.*

I can't. I killed my mother. I hurt you.

It was all a lie.

But I saw it. I saw her.

How could you see anything after you were attacked?

He paused. *She was there. I remember that...and they told me I may have...poor Mum.*

It wasn't you.

And you...I saw you. The fear you had.

I've never been afraid of you. You are not a beast. Someone else hurt your mother and when you hurt me that night you were only fighting a dream.

But the prophesy?

Only you can stop it from coming true.

Me?

Yes.

How?

You must live. You might fight the darkness and come back to me.

CHAPTER 52

Angela was scared. She stared out the window at the crowds leisurely passing her hotel suite. The summer sun high in the sky.

Her husband had taken her out of London for a while to 'steady' her nerves. But the trip to Paris had done nothing. Angela sent a cursory glance at the shopping bags she'd left on the couch. The staff would later pack them away; right now she wanted to think. Fortunately, she was alone; her husband had taken the girls out shopping.

Angela covered her mouth and fought the building of tears in her eyes. With Joanna gone there was no one to talk to. Not the way she needed to. She missed the tea and biscuits. She never thought she would have, but she did. But most of all she missed Joanna. Joanna understood what a mother sacrificed. What a mother's role was supposed to be.

She'd done it all for Cory and for her girls. It was a mother's duty to protect her children's future. Graham had promised her that he could control James. Keep him in line. Make sure that he stayed out of the picture long enough for Cory to shine. Having

James tucked away on St. Clarine in that shabby mansion had been ideal. Since the loss of his mother and his sight, James showed little interest in the business anymore.

But then Martha had to interfere and call *that* girl. Her husband had no idea how her blood boiled while she listened to the hope in his voice that Michelle would be able to lure James back into the fold. That they could cajole him to use his brilliant mind again. What about your son? Your daughters? She wanted to shout at him. But she only smiled and planned.

She never thought Michelle would go. It had been too long and from what she understood, he had left her. Didn't the woman have any pride? Plain as she was didn't she know it was better to wait for a man to come to her?

But when Graham had called her and told her what the woman he'd placed at James's place had said, she knew she had to do something. Graham said he'd take care of it. Graham always took care of things. Joanna had trusted him.

Graham had gone too far this time. The allegations were damming. But if he said anything, she'd deny it. She'd paid him in cash. Their communication had been short and she'd known him for years, it was perfectly reasonable that she'd converse with him. Her husband wouldn't believe it and neither would Martha. Besides, Angela was a Winfield and they protected each other. No matter what.

A BLOODLINE ISN'T TAINTED, only the mind is.

Teresa's words haunted Kenneth until late the next day. He and Jessie had left the hospital, offering Teresa and Sean a place to stay before heading back home. Now it was wait and see. Kenneth still couldn't fathom all that he'd heard in the hospital waiting room. He couldn't believe all that the Winfields had done. Had hidden.

Just like his family had.

But James had been more optimistic than Kenneth had ever been. He remembered being at their wedding reception and envying the older man's joy. He didn't think it was possible. He'd been hiding his own secrets back then. But now that was over.

Kenneth didn't sleep well thinking about Michelle, hoping James pulled through and pondering Teresa's words. He slept in late and woke to his son's wailing. Instead of turning over in bed as he usually did, Kenneth followed the sound of the cries, and made his way to the kitchen where he saw Joyce trying to soothe a crying Alex whose nose was as red as a cherry.

"I'm sorry," he heard Syrah say.

"Accidents happen." Joyce replied.

"What accident?" Kenneth said.

Syrah turned to him looking miserable. "I opened a cupboard to get a glass just as Joyce was passing with Alex—"

"And it hit him in the face," Joyce finished, bouncing the screaming baby on her hip. "I'm sure he'll calm down in a minute."

"I'm so sorry, Dad. I know I should have been more careful."

"It's okay," Kenneth said, affectionately patting her on the head before he turned to Joyce. He took a deep breath then said, "Hand him to me."

She gaped at him as if he'd suddenly levitated. Syrah did too.

Kenneth couldn't stop a smile at the sight of their startled faces. He reached for Alex. "Go on. Hand him over."

Joyce blinked and did so. And Alex continued to wail, even curling his back to let out his baby rage, but Kenneth felt calm. Almost happy. "Go ahead and cry little one," he said. "Life hurts, but I've got you." He didn't know what he was saying or doing, but the words felt right and he wasn't going to stop holding him. Kenneth held Alex's head, caressed his hot, tear stained cheek, and stroked his back, knowing his own father had never held him this way.

There was never tenderness in his father's touch. Only pain. But he wasn't his father or his brother and Alex's past would be different than his. And Kenneth remembered the man who he considered his true father, a man who had given him his name and taught him how to love. A man who he wanted to make proud. Kenneth took a deep breath and inhaled Alex's soft baby scent, brushed his chin against the tight curls on his head. Kenneth's heart filled with love and a desire to protect. No matter what Alex did, he knew he'd never hurt him. He wasn't that kind of man. The cycle was broken.

Soon Alex's cries settled into whimpers, then hiccups, and then drifted into silence. Kenneth felt his son's warm breath on his neck and looked down to see that he'd fallen asleep.

"He's never done that after a temper," Joyce said amazed.

"You're a natural, Dad," Syrah said.

Kenneth glanced up to tease that he'd just gotten lucky when he saw Jessie standing in the entryway. She had tears in her eyes. Tears of joy. He swallowed a lump in his throat, sorry he'd hurt her because of his fears.

"Jasmine, I—" he began, but she rushed over and kissed him on the cheek and said, "I know."

CHAPTER 53

He remembered her voice. He remembered Michelle's voice calling him, drawing him back from the edge of the abyss.

He could break the curse, she said.

He could be with her, she said.

At last.

James opened his eyes and although he saw mostly shadows, he immediately knew where he was. He'd woken up in enough hospitals to identify them by the sound of rubber soles against the tiled floors and wheeled beds rolling down a corridor; the scent of flowers and medicine. He felt a hand in his, a soft female hand, and closed his hand around it.

He heard her gasp, and for a moment, briefly, he wished he could see her face again. He'd been told a couple of years ago that his optic nerve hadn't been permanently damaged and with surgery he could possibly regain partial vision, some of the shadows would remain but he would see a little more light. However, nothing was certain and after his mother's death, he had felt his current state was well deserved. He still wasn't sure he wanted more surgeries. For now the fact that Michelle was there—he could feel her, hear her, inhale her scent—was enough.

"You're awake," Michelle said. "Let me get a nurse."

He shook his head. "Not yet."

"But—"

"Not yet, please." *Are we alone?* He silently asked her.

Yes.

Was it a dream?

No. It's finally over. You didn't kill Joanna. It seems she surprised the attackers and—

But Gran said I might have—

"You were too injured to do anything. It was Graham who tried to suggest otherwise because he wanted to get back at you for running off and marrying me without him knowing.

James nodded. That made sense. Graham hadn't been the man he thought he was. The incident in St. Clarine had taught him that.

Michelle held James's hand and watched his face settle into understanding. She'd agreed with Martha that he'd never need to know the full truth about his mother and, in turn, her own involvement. Her marriage and business were safe now. Martha could never threaten her again and Michelle knew James's uncles would lookout for his future in the company. They too would keep whatever they knew from him, although Martha had kept them in the dark as well.

Michelle had learned that darkness had its uses. She would lie in order not to cause James anymore pain. There was no need to shine a light on the truth. Stories have power. It was something her father used to always tell them. Now she knew how much.

With her free hand, Michelle lightly stroked his cheek. "Let me call the nurse now."

James covered her hand then frowned as he realized something was missing. "Where's your ring?"

"I exchanged it for something much more precious—you."

"Me?"

"Yes, I'll tell you the story someday." She kissed him on the lips then whispered. "Now I'm calling a nurse."

The hospital was astounded by James's recovering but put him under observation for one more day just to be safe. However, they allowed him to see visitors. And James was pleasantly surprised to have more than he'd expected, he'd only expected his grandmother and uncles who were stateside, but more well-wishers arrived.

"It's me, Teresa," a familiar voice said, placing a kiss on his cheek. "And this is my husband, Sean."

"A pleasure," Sean said, holding out his hand.

James's hand fumbled in the air a bit before he found and shook Sean's hand. "Likewise." He drew away then suddenly felt another solid male hand take his and offer a friendly, confident shake. "I'm Kenneth Preston, Jasmine's husband."

James lifted his brows. "Your name sounds exactly the same as the guy she used to hate."

"I *am* the guy she used to hate."

"Not anymore," Jessie said with laughter in her voice. They introduced him to their daughter and son and James felt the warmth of the family he'd always wanted to be a part of. He was sorry to hear about the Clifton's passing, but knew they'd be pleased their daughters were doing well. He knew his own mother would feel the same.

On the day of his release, outside the hospital doors, James felt the humid heat that reminded him of their wedding day. In his memory he saw his new bride standing beside him. He felt Michelle wrap her arm around him, just as she had in the castle garden and made him feel strong and offered him a new future. "Where do we go from here?" she asked him.

Anywhere and everywhere, he wanted to say, but instead he said the words he knew she wanted to hear, "We go home."

He'd always felt special. Even at the orphanage he felt different from the rest. When he was finally adopted by a kind couple—a porter and former school teacher—and given his permanent name, Stanford Norman, he knew in his heart how lucky he was.

He also knew his passion. Clothes. He didn't know why the sound of the sewing machine filled him with such calm and joy. It gave him a sense of home. He begged his mother to show him how to use it and pestered her until she did. Then he couldn't stay away. His parents silently worried about him, but they didn't interfere.

He designed his mother's dresses, his father's shirts, his sister's costumes. He learned about color, texture and lines.

Deep in his bones he knew who he was and what he was meant for; he didn't care how the world saw him because ever since he could remember, he'd always felt a great love had formed him.

That a great love had raised him.

And through his international company, where he designed and crafted ethnically embellished clothing, he shared that great love with the world.

ABOUT THE AUTHOR

Dara Girard, an award-winning, national bestselling author of more than forty novels, from romance to suspense, loves telling stories.

Born in the US to immigrant parents, Dara enjoys pulling from her Jamaican, British, Nigerian heritage and exposure to various cultures to bring what reviewers and fans call "vivid emotional stories" to life. She is best known for her popular Henson Series, the mysterious Clifton Sisters, and the fun Black Stockings Society.

You can write her at:
contactdara@daragirard.com
or
P.O. Box 10345
Silver Spring, MD 20914
If you'd like to receive a reply, please send a self-addressed stamped envelope.

Visit her website to sign up for her newsletter and get sneak peeks, monthly updates on new releases, and special offers.

For more information visit
www.daragirard.com

DARA GIRARD

The Amber Stone

A CLIFTON SISTER NOVEL

www.ingramcontent.com/pod-product-compliance
Lightning Source LLC
Chambersburg PA
CBHW030018200726
48283CB00012B/678